Deadly Choices:

Tales of Deceit and Revenge

by
Bobby J Watson

The Bully | The Perfect Plan | One Stupid Mistake

Friday Night Lights | Revenge

This book is a work of fiction. Names, characters, places, and incidents are the product of the author's imagination or are used fictitiously. Any resemblance to actual events, locales, or persons, living or dead, is coincidental and not intended by the author.

ISBN: 979-8-9877831-4-6

Printed in the United States of America

Table of Contents

*This book is dedicated to
my brother Ray Watson
who loves a good crime story*

The Bully

by
Bobby J Watson

We are only falsehood, duplicity, contradiction; we both conceal and disguise ourselves from ourselves.

-Blaise Pascal

CHAPTER ONE

Amanda was working on her laptop in her home office when she heard the front door open and slam shut. She knew something was wrong right away. Her son Jonathan had arrived home from school, but he never slammed the door like that. She got up from her desk and rushed to his room where she found him lying on his bed, sobbing with tears running down both cheeks. He turned away when he saw her, but she sat down on the edge of the bed and said "Johnny look at me. What's wrong?" When he didn't respond she gently took him by the shoulders and pulled him toward her. It was then that she saw the blood, some matted on his upper lip and a thick stream congealing on his nose.

"Johnny! What happened? Who did this?" But even as she screamed she knew the answer. "Did Max do this to you?" Johnny looked at her and slowly nodded his head.

Max was the child next door. He and his parents had lived there when Amanda and her husband Michael had bought their house twelve years ago. They were newlyweds at the time and it was their first, and so far, their only home. They had met Connor and Jessica and their newborn Max soon after moving into the house. The two houses sat at the end of a cul-de-sac on a quiet street. Jessica had welcomed them with an apple pie as a house-warming gift and was very friendly. She had even offered Amanda some suggestions on local shops for furnishings and home décor. Connor was more reserved but seemed friendly enough.

Things changed a few months later when Jessica was hit by a drunk driver and seriously injured in a car accident. Michael and Amanda had visited her in the hospital, but she was in a coma in ICU and never recovered. She died six days after the accident, leaving Connor a widower with an infant to raise. To his credit he hired a nanny and seemed to be trying his best to fulfill his role as a single parent. But the tragedy had obviously left him emotionally scarred. He became more reclusive and when you engaged him in conversation he seldom had more than a one word answer.

A year and half later Amanda gave birth to Jonathan. Both she and Michael were thrilled and threw themselves into being the best parents they could be. As both boys grew older she and the nanny would sometimes chat and take the boys to the park together. Max and Johnny got along well together, but it was obvious that Max, being older, was the leader. He would make suggestions as they pretended to be super heroes or pirates or soldiers or whatever.

When Max started elementary school, Connor transitioned to a job where he could work from home two or three days a week and in the office the other days. Then when Max entered fourth grade, Connor let the nanny go and Max stayed home alone on the days Connor was in the office. Amanda would never have allowed this with Johnny, but it was only for two or three hours and appeared to work okay. Michael and Amanda noted that Connor seemed to become even more reclusive as time went by, and his attitude when they did engage him in conversation was often very harsh and even hateful toward everything. This apparently affected Max as well. His playing with Johnny got rougher and more reckless and reached a point where Johnny didn't want to play with him. Amanda and Michael saw the changes also and didn't encourage them to play together.

When Johnny started school, Amanda would take him and pick him up in the afternoon. But this year he was ten years old and at his request she allowed him to walk home with other neighborhood kids in the afternoon unless the weather was too bad. This had worked well, except there had been a couple of previous incidents where Max had bullied him when just the two of them walked up their cul-de-sac.

Now as she cleaned the blood off of Johnny's nose and doctored the wound, she was steaming. How could she let this go and do nothing? Tears rolled down her cheeks even as she wiped Johnny's tears off of his own cheeks. She wanted to march over and bang on Connor's door and tell him what a thug he was raising. She wanted to tell him what an insensitive and thoughtless father he was and what a poor job he was doing. She wanted to tell him that she was going to call the school and report Max's behavior so they could make sure he didn't hurt any other kids.

All of these thoughts ran through her mind, but as she comforted Johnny she also wanted to stay right there and hug him and tell him how much she loved him. She told him that none of this was his fault and she would see that Max never hurt him again. She told him that she and his dad would talk to Max's father and make sure that Max stayed away from him.

Once she had collected herself and gotten better control of her emotions she decided to wait until Michael came home. He should be home soon. She would tell him what Max had done and let him talk to Connor. It was probably best to let them talk man to man.

CHAPTER TWO

Michael sat in a corner table at The Dugout Sports Bar and Grill nursing a draft beer. It was about 4:30 in the afternoon and the bar was starting to get more business as people got off work and stopped in for a drink before going home. He recognized a number of familiar faces and saw different groups form and chat and laugh as they enjoyed their brews. A basketball game was playing on two screens and a replay of a late-season college football game from the previous week played on another couple of screens. Michael paid them no attention, though the crowd would occasionally roar as someone scored or stole the ball in the basketball game. He wasn't much of a sports fan, but he enjoyed the solitude that prevailed in the bar until the after-work onslaught started.

Michael had been out of work for six months now. He had been laid off from his job when another company acquired the business where he worked and laid off a significant number of the senior staff. He had received a severance package at the time but had also gone through a brief period of depression. Nobody likes to feel like they are no longer needed and it hit him especially hard. Fortunately Amanda made a higher salary than he did and so after the severance dried up, they were able to stay afloat.

After the first month of being laid off he had updated his resume and started looking for his next opportunity. He enrolled in several job-search websites and went on a number of interviews. At first things looked promising. Two of his interviews seemed like they would lead to job offers but then they fizzled out. A third company did offer him a job, but the pay was so much lower that his pride simply wouldn't allow him to accept it.

This went on for three or four months and he became less and less confident that a job would come along. Actually he started feeling quite depressed again, but he refused to let Amanda see it. Instead he fabricated stories about interviews and left home almost every day, either to attend interviews that didn't exist or to talk to a job placement advisor who also didn't exist. These trips always took him to The Dugout Sports Bar and Grill where he sat in the corner and watched the other customers as he sipped on a draft beer. He told himself that next week or next month would be different and he would again get serious and find a good job. After all he had a college degree and years of prior experience. Unfortunately, next week or next month never came.

He now looked at the time on his iPhone and saw that it was almost 5:00 PM. The bar was getting more crowded and was no longer the quiet refuge that he enjoyed. He knew that Amanda would be expecting him and he would have to dream up some encouraging progress to report to her. When he stopped and thought about it, he was sometimes amazed that he had been lucky enough to meet and marry her. She was a perfect wife and mother and he loved her dearly. She seemed to never get discouraged with his situation but instead was always positive that things would turn around soon.

Johnny might also need some help with his homework when he got home. It was common for them to do homework together while Amanda wrapped up her work for the day and prepared dinner for three of them. Johnny was a bright boy and Michael loved being with him and helping him do his homework. If there was little or no homework, they would talk about their next adventure. The two of them would spend a few weekends every year camping and fishing. He loved to fish and had taught Johnny from an early age the art of angling. They both loved it and half the fun was planning their next location and next trip.

Yes, it was time to go home. And next week he was going to get serious again about finding a job. This couldn't go on forever.

CHAPTER THREE

Michael pulled into his driveway and noticed that Connor's red pickup truck was in his driveway. *Must have worked at home today, or maybe he just got home* he mused to himself. As he got out of his car he saw old man Gallagher across the street. The old man and his wife were the third and final house on their cul-de-sac. They had been the first people to buy a home in the neighborhood when it was first developed. Mrs. Gallagher used to work diligently in their garden, thinning weeds and planting annual flowers. But now as she had aged she seldom got out of the house. The old man had let the flower garden go, but was now raking leaves from the large oak tree that sat in the center of their front lawn.

He waved and walked over toward Michael. Michael didn't really care for a conversation but walked to the center of the street and spoke to the old man. They exchanged hellos and chatted for a few minutes. The old man commented that Connor's house could use a paint job and he hated to see him bringing down the appearance of their street. He also seemed to let his lawn go without raking up all the dead leaves. Michael agreed with the old man and wondered to himself if Gallagher thought he and Amanda were also negligent homeowners. He then quickly made an excuse and headed toward his front door.

Amanda had heard the car pull into the driveway and was waiting for Michael inside the front door. She didn't want to go outside and make a scene so she waited impatiently at the door. When Michael opened it and walked in, she unloaded on him.

"That little bully Max is at it again, Michael! He gave Johnny a bloody nose on their walk home from school today! I want you to go over there right now and talk to his dad. If he can't control that boy, I'm going to report him to the police and I'm notifying the school too. It's just isn't right! Johnny can't even feel safe on his own street because of that bully. Now go over there right now and talk to him."

"Whoa, hold on Amanda. Where's Johnny? In his room? I want to see him. Is he okay? Did you call a doctor?"

"He's in his room. No, I didn't call a doctor. I was able to take care of it myself."

Michael walked into his son's room and found him lying on his bed. He had quit crying but his eyes were blood red and his nose was starting to develop a small bruised spot. He sat down on the edge of the bed beside his son.

"Hey buddy, what happened?"

"Max just slugged me for no reason."

"Had you two been arguing or anything? What brought it on?"

"Nothing Daddy, I swear. We just started up our street and he started calling me a wimp and shoving my shoulder. I told him to quit and he said 'make me, wimp' and I shoved him back and started walking faster. He ran up and grabbed my arm and swung me around and hit me in the nose. It started bleeding. I could taste the blood, and he just started laughing and calling me names."

"That's all? You're not leaving anything out?"

"That's all, Daddy. I promise."

"Okay, well you lay here and rest. It's going to be okay. I promise."

He got up from the bed and saw Amanda in the doorway.

"Okay, I'll go over and talk to Connor" he said and rushed toward the door.

Connor opened the door on the second ring of the doorbell. He looked annoyed to see Michael but greeted him, "Hi Michael, what's shaking?"

"What's shaking? Your son, Connor. That's what's shaking. He punched Johnny on their walk home today and gave him a bloody nose. You've got to do something about him. I'm sick and tired of him bullying my son."

"Oh good grief, Michael. Boys are going to be boys. They get into scuffles. You know that."

"This wasn't a scuffle. He hit Johnny for no reason and with no warning."

"Max, get in here! And I mean now!"

Max walked in the room looking as unconcerned and innocent as he could possibly look and said, "What's up, Pop?"

"Michael here says that you beat up his kid today for no reason. Is that true? And don't lie to me, boy."

"Well, we got into it a little but he hit me first. I was just defending myself. I didn't want to hurt him."

Michael asked, "What did you get into it about?"

"Something stupid is all. He called me a dummy because I made a "C" on a spelling test and he said anybody with a brain could do better than that." Max said this with a visible smirk that practically shouted that he was making it up as he told it.

"That's a lie. He told me you hit him for no reason."

"Don't call my boy a liar, Michael! You leave now. You might want to go home and teach little Johnny some boxing lessons. Toughen him up a little."

"I'm going to say this once Connor and you listen too Max. If my boy gets hurt one more time, there's gonna be a price to pay and you two are paying it."

"Yeah, yeah. You're probably as big a wimp as your kid. Now it's time for you to leave."

Michael went back to his own house and told Amanda about the exchange he had with Connor and Max. He then went into Johnny's room and questioned him about the spelling test grade. Johnny told him that was a lie and said once again that Max hit him for no reason. He believed his son.

"They're both liars!" Amanda screamed.

"I know, I know. Let's just hope they got the message."

Amanda hoped that they had gotten the message, but she had no real confidence in that. In her mind they were both bullies. She would drive Johnny to and from school the next few days and maybe things would simmer down.

CHAPTER FOUR

So for the rest of that week and the following week she drove Johnny to school and picked him up afterward also. He didn't go outside to play, just stayed in the house watching TV and playing video games when he wasn't doing his homework. But as the days passed that second week he became more and more anxious to start walking home again with his friends. He missed not walking with them, but more than that he was embarrassed and didn't want them to know why he wasn't walking with them. He made up different excuses to explain why his mom was picking him up, and he was running out of reasons. He didn't want them to know that Max had beat him up and he was scared of him.

After hearing him beg to walk for a few days, Amanda finally gave in and allowed him to walk home again. She stood in their front yard and watched as he walked up their street, making sure that Max didn't attack him. This lasted for another week or two and then she finally slacked off. Perhaps by now Max had learned his lesson and knew better than to pick on her son. But no, that wasn't the case. Just a few days after she relaxed her vigilance Johnny came home visibly upset.

"Johnny, what's wrong? Has Max hurt you?"

He shook his head from side to side and said "No".

"Then what is it?"

Finally Johnny calmed down and told her that Max had called him names and told him he was a stupid idiot and a wimp. He had walked alongside him and yelled one obscene name after another into his ear. Then when Johnny started crying, Max began laughing and telling him what a baby he was. "Go cry to your mommy, baby" he had taunted him.

Amanda looked outside and saw that Connor was home. She told Johnny to stay there and she practically ran over to their house and banged on the door.

"Open this door, Connor! I mean now!"

Connor opened the door and she flew into his entryway.

"Where's that little bully of yours? I want to talk to him right now!"

"Settle down, Amanda. Good grief, what's wrong now?"

"What's wrong is that I'm sick and tired of your boy making mine miserable, picking on him and hitting him and terrorizing him. I want it stopped."

Connor called the boy into the room and he of course denied everything.

"You're a pathetic little liar" she shouted at him. "Connor, I want this stopped now. I don't want Max near my boy. I don't want him talking with him. I don't want him walking up the street with him. I want him to stay away from Johnny. Do you understand? Because if you don't I'm calling the police."

"Now now, settle down Amanda. We can work this out. Boys are always butting heads and arguing. That's just part of being a boy. But I'm going to talk with Max and I'll make sure he stays away from your kid. They obviously don't get along. And Max I want you to just stay away from Johnny. He's an overly sensitive little guy and just can't take a little jostling. You hear me?"

16

"Sure dad, I'll stay away from him."

"Okay Amanda, you satisfied? There's no need to get police involved. We can handle this ourselves."

"I'll be satisfied when I'm sure Max is doing what you told him to do. But I warn you if there's any more trouble, I'm doing something. I'm calling the police, the school, whoever I have to call to end this."

She then stormed out the door, slamming it behind her.

Connor then turned to Max. "Emotional little thing isn't she. Just leave the boy alone. I don't care whose fault it is, just leave him alone. I don't need this. Now go on back to your room."

Amanda went back home and retreated to her bedroom. She shut the door and sat on her bed. She began to shake and then the tears started rolling down her cheeks. No mother can see her only child tormented and just let it go. She was at the end of her rope and couldn't take anymore. And it wasn't just the situation with Max. That was bad enough, but she was engaged in a difficult project at work that was driving her mad. The clients on this particular project were very demanding and never satisfied. She was stressed out. Then on top of that Michael was still out of work and looking for a job. He had told her that he was going to a nearby suburb for another interview today. She would have preferred that he deal with Connor and Max. Everything was building up and up and she felt she would explode if it got any worse.

She said a silent prayer that Connor would really control Max this time and then she went back into the living room. She held Johnny and comforted him and told him yet again that everything would be okay.

CHAPTER FIVE

And everything was alright, for the rest of that week. Johnny walked home from school with his friends and up the cul-de-sac to their house. Amanda was in the yard each day watching and waiting. Max was walking alongside him each day and even waved at Amanda as he headed towards his own front door. Amanda didn't wave, but she did nod her head at him to acknowledge his wave. Johnny said that Max was actually being very nice to him, talking about school and sports and other stuff. Amanda reacted positively to this news, but secretly she knew it was just an act that Max was putting on for her benefit. She still didn't trust the kid.

Her distrust was confirmed on Tuesday of the following week. Johnny came home crying yet again. Amanda had been waiting in the front yard again that day, but got an urgent text from work and had to go inside to use her laptop in response to the text. Johnny came in the door and she heard him crying and immediately left her computer and ran to meet him. He had a black eye and a small cut on his chin where he had obviously been hit. She dashed to the medicine cabinet and began patching up his chin and applying an ice bag to his eye. She was beginning to feel like a corner man in a boxing ring.

Once she had finished doctoring her son, she asked what happened this time. "Max and I were nearly home and he saw that you weren't waiting for me and he said 'oh, mommy's not waiting for her baby boy today'. I told him not to start bothering me and he just kept teasing me and then he shoved me down to the ground. I got up, and mom I couldn't take anymore so I took a swing at him. I missed but then he beat me up and started laughing and calling me wimp and baby and all sorts of names. I'm sorry mom."

"You don't have to be sorry, Johnny. You did nothing wrong. But I've had it too. You wait here. I'm going to go over there and settle this thing, and right now."

She stormed out the door before Johnny could say anything else. He didn't want Max to hurt his mom, but he stayed there like she had told him to do.

Amanda took long strides in a walk-run towards Max's door. She didn't check if Connor was home or not and she really didn't care. She approached the door and beat on it and then tried the door knob. Max had failed to lock the door. She burst in and called his name. "Max! Where are you? Come here right now!"

Max came out of the kitchen and said, "My dad's not home now. You need to leave." He then turned and went back into the kitchen.

Amanda followed him into the kitchen and responded, "I don't care if he's home or not. You're going to listen to me this time young man!"

"I don't know what Johnny told you, but I was just defending myself. He took a swing at me. I had to defend myself."

"Yeah he told me. After you called him names and shoved him to the ground."

"That's a lie! He just swung at me for no reason. Probably thought you'd be in the front yard and I wouldn't do anything in front of his mommy."

"Cut the crap, Max. You're the liar and we both know it."

What happened after that was a blur. Everything slowed down for Amanda and it was like she was in a dream or another world. She charged Max and slapped him right in the face. Max reached for a carving knife that was lying on the kitchen counter and backed away from her. He held the knife in his fist like he would stab her if she came closer. But Amanda came anyway and kicked him in the shin. He screamed in pain and she grabbed the knife out of his hand. He doubled his fist and she knew he was going to hit her, so she swung the knife at him. He backed away from her.

"What's the matter, Max? You a wimp? Daddy not here to protect you?"

Max was now scared and started to cry and crumbled into a sitting position in the corner of the room.

"Please, let me go. I promise I won't ever hurt Johnny again. I promise."

"No, Max. You can't help it. You're a bully and you just can't help yourself. And I can't keep letting you hurt my boy."

With that she came right up to him and bent down and stabbed Max in the neck. Blood exploded everywhere. She stabbed him again, and again, and again. She didn't know how many times she hit him with the knife as she took out all of her pent up rage, fear, and frustration on him. She finally quit and started getting control of herself as Max lay lifeless in the corner.

Now what? Connor might come home at any moment. What should she do? She had blood all over her blouse and some on her jeans. She only knew one thing to do and she fished her cell phone out of her rear pocket and called Michael. He answered on the second ring and said, "I'm nearly home, hon. Be there in five minutes."

"Oh Michael! I've done something terribly wrong!"

Michael didn't hear everything as his phone connection became spotty but he could tell that Amanda was terribly upset. He hoped Johnny had not gotten hurt again. His connection improved again and he couldn't believe what he heard next.

"Michael! I've killed Max. I'm at his house now. Please! What should I do?"

CHAPTER SIX

Michael couldn't believe what his ears had heard. "What did you say?"

"I killed Max! He beat Johnny up again and I just went crazy. I came over here and he tried to deny it and I just lost it. He grabbed a knife and I took it away from him and stabbed him. I couldn't take anymore. I just lost it."

"You're there now? You stabbed him and he's dead?"

"Yes, it just happened and I called you." He could hear the hysteria in her voice.

"Are you sure he's dead? Maybe he's not and you can call an ambulance."

"No, Michael. Listen to me. He's dead. I know it. I went crazy for a few seconds and stabbed him over and over. I've got blood all over me. He's dead."

"Oh my God. I can't believe this." He pulled over into a grocery store parking lot and took a deep breath. He tried to think what to do. One thing came to his mind over and over: I must protect Amanda and Johnny.

"Okay, I want you to leave now. Make sure no one is outside. No neighbors. Then run to the house and get those clothes off. Put them in a trash bag or something and take a shower. Try to not let Johnny see you."

"Okay, what are you going to do?"

"I don't know. I'm going to clean it up so they don't know you were there. Just do what I say."

Amanda did as Michael said. She peeked out the door and saw that the street was empty. Then she sprinted to their house and ran inside. She didn't see Johnny and ran straight towards the bathroom. She threw a large bath towel on the floor and piled the bloody clothes on it as she stripped. She locked the door. Johnny would never try to come in while she was showering, but she locked it anyway just to be sure. She then stepped into a hot steaming shower and scrubbed her body and her hair like she had never done before. The hot shower was surprisingly comforting as she washed and slowly settled her nerves.

After drying off, she put on clean clothes and went to the laundry room to retrieve a trash bag. On the way she looked in on Johnny and saw that he was playing a virtual reality game and was lost in his own little world. She worried about his playing those games too much, but today she couldn't have been happier to see him playing and swinging his arms, probably emulating rock climbing which was one of his favorite games. She got the bag and retreated to the bathroom where she stuffed the clothes and towel into the bag.

Michael drove the remaining blocks to his house with his mind in a fog. He tried to think what to do and thought about police shows he had watched, but everything was like a dream. He arrived at home and put the car in the garage. He looked around the street and seeing it empty, he walked briskly to Connor's house. His thoughts began to crystallize. He knew that Connor would be home soon so he would have to work fast. Opening the front door he walked straight to the kitchen where he saw Max lying in the corner. There was no way he could remove the body or get rid of all the blood. There simply wasn't enough time. He saw the bloody knife on the floor and he took his handkerchief and picked it up. He wiped back and forth along the handle several times, hopefully erasing any fingerprints. He thought it would be logical for a thief to wear gloves and leave no prints. Looking around more, he didn't see anything else that needed removal or cleaning and stuffed the handkerchief in his coat pocket. His or Amanda's fingerprints might be in the living room but they could explain that. After all they were neighbors and had been in the house.

He prepared to leave and then had another thought. He went to the front door and locked it. It was one of those combination locks that makes you enter a four-digit code to unlock or lock it. Soon after they had moved in Connor and Jessica had gone on vacation and had given the code to him and Amanda so they could feed the cat that they owned at the time. Michael was good with numbers and remembered the code, not that remembering 4-3-2-1 was that difficult.

He then ran to their back door which was locked, went outside, and crashed through it, making it look like someone had broken into the house and been surprised to find Max there. He then exited the back yard and went to his own house where he found Amanda anxiously awaiting him. He took the trash bag from her, and after placing his bloody handkerchief in the bag, he took it to the only place that came to mind: the city dump. The dump was open on weekdays until 6:00 PM and he got there at 5:55. After showing his license to prove his residency he tossed the bag onto a heap of other bags, broken furniture and miscellaneous junk and returned home.

By the time he arrived home Connor had already shown up and made the awful discovery. He was sitting on his front step and police were coming in and out of the house. There were three police cars, a police van and an ambulance in front of the house. Michael looked at Connor and couldn't begin to imagine what the man must be feeling. He had lost his wife, and now his son. His life was shattered. It would never be the same. Michael started to walk over to him, but then thought better of it. There were neighbors who had walked up to the bubble at the end of cul-de-sac, taking in the tragic scene. He saw old man Gallagher in his front yard, staring at him and at the scene, and started to walk over to him but again had second thoughts and instead retreated into his own house. He wasn't sure he could act shocked and surprised enough and deemed it better to just not speak to anyone.

Amanda met him inside and ran and hugged him like never before. Max was not a good kid but they had tried all they knew to do to solve that problem. Nothing had worked, but that didn't make this right. Max should still be alive. Connor should still have a son. But as he wrapped his arms around Amanda and comforted her, he believed he had done what he need to do. He had protected his family.

CHAPTER SEVEN

The knock on the door came about twenty minutes later. Michael looked at Amanda as if to say *okay it's about to start* and then opened the door. Officer Jennings from the police department asked if he could come in and ask them a few questions. He explained that there had been a break-in next door and a young boy had been killed. Amanda gasped and said, "Oh my God! You mean Max has been killed!" Michael tried to emulate her stellar performance, "Are you sure? I can't believe that, not in our neighborhood!"

"I'm afraid so" said Officer Jennings. Then he added, "So you know the family?"

"Oh, yes. We've lived next door to each other for years. Max and our own son have grown up together."

"I see. Well, we're asking all the neighbors if they saw anything or anyone suspicious. Did you see anyone knocking on their door, or in their back yard?"

"No" Amanda said. "I really have been busy on the computer all day. I work at home and have been inside all day."

"I just got home myself about twenty minutes ago" added Michael. "The police and ambulance were all here when I pulled in the drive."

"Okay, you said your son and Max were friends. Could we ask him these same questions?"

"Oh, I'd rather not disturb him. He came home from school not feeling well and is asleep in his room. I'm sure if he saw anything like that he would have mentioned it."

"Very well. If you could just ask him anyway when he wakes up and call us if he did see something or if you think of anything else. Here's the phone number for the lead detective on the case" Jennings said and handed Amanda a business card.

"Yes, we sure will. I hope you find whoever did this."

Jennings left and Amanda collapsed unto the sofa. "I just can't believe this. What have I done?"

"It's not a question of what you've done anymore. It's a question of surviving to keep our family together. I'm going to go shower. I don't think I have any blood or anything on me but we can't take a chance. My clothes should be okay too, but put them in the wash right now, just to be safe."

"I will, and Michael thank you for being so supportive. I know this isn't easy for you" she said as he headed to the bathroom.

Things seemed to settle down a little bit after that. After Michael showered they went into Johnny's room and found him doing his homework. Michael looked at his band-aided chin and black eye and told Johnny it should all be well in a few days. They then told him what had happened next door. A burglar had broken into Connor and Max's house and apparently been surprised to find Max there. They told him that Max was dead and police were trying to find the person who did it. Johnny was shocked and couldn't believe it.

Amanda asked him, "You didn't see anyone strange on the street or around their house did you?"

"No, but I was just running home after Max hit me. I didn't see anything."

"I didn't think so, but I told the police officer I would ask you."

Amanda then prepared dinner for them. She put a frozen meatloaf meal from the supermarket in the oven and warmed some corn and green beans to go with it. It was later than usual when they ate due to the circumstances and after dinner they told Johnny to take his bath and get ready for bed. He asked if he had to go to school tomorrow and they told him that they would discuss that in the morning.

They tried to settle in on the sofa and watch a movie after that, but neither of them could focus on it. Amanda kept questioning how well Michael had cleaned up and he explained his actions over and over again. He thought that everything was taken care of and they would not be able to tie anything back to them, but they could never be completely sure. In his own mind Michael wondered what he would do if they arrested some innocent person. Could he let someone else pay for a crime that he and his wife had committed?

The answer to that came two days later on Thursday with a loud knock on the door at 7:00 AM. Johnny had skipped school on Wednesday but was dressed and eating breakfast before returning to school when the knock came. Amanda was still in her bathrobe, having fixed Johnny's cereal and orange juice. She was about to change into her clothes when the knock came. Michael had awakened about 6:00 AM, gotten dressed, and was watching one of the local morning news shows when the knock came.

He opened the door to see a man in a suit with a white shirt and tie. Behind him stood two police officers, one of them being Officer Jennings.

The suit asked "Are you Michael Woodson?" Michael replied that yes he was and the man said "I'm Detective Davies. Michael Woodson, you're under arrest for the murder of Max Gibson." He then read Michael his rights and asked him to turn around.

"No, no" Michael said. "I didn't do that. You've got it all wrong."

"We don't think so but that's for the D.A. and the courts to work out."

Amanda heard the commotion and rushed into the room, followed by Johnny. She couldn't believe what was happening. Johnny was scared and beside himself.

"That's my daddy! He didn't hurt anyone. Don't take him!"

The detective told Amanda that Michael would be booked in the downtown police station. Michael shouted for her to get him a lawyer as they escorted him out the door.

CHAPTER EIGHT

Everything seemed to be happening at breakneck speed after that, though in reality it took several months. Amanda took Johnny to her mother's house and explained the situation to her. Her mother was a retired nurse in her late seventies and thought the world of Michael. She couldn't believe that he would harm anyone, much less kill a young boy. She said that surely someone would come forward and say they witnessed the break-in or the person who did it would make a mistake. God just wouldn't allow this injustice to happen. She and Johnny had a close relationship and Amanda knew that if anyone could comfort her son, it would be her mother.

She then went back home and began searching for an attorney. She had no knowledge of criminal attorneys in their area and didn't know anyone who might offer advice. She finally settled on one she found on the internet who had good reviews and called his office. He told her to meet him downtown at the police station. Michael was booked and spent the next two days in the county jail before being arraigned. At the arraignment he was charged with second degree murder and burglary to which he pled not guilty. Bail was set at one million dollars and Amanda had to use money from her 401(k) to put up the $100,000 that was required. Michael was relieved, scared and exhausted all at the same time and anxious to get home.

He began meeting regularly with the defense attorney, Benjamin White, after that as they planned their strategy. He told White that he had been at The Dugout Sports Bar and Grill until late that afternoon and, although he hadn't spoken to anyone there, they found witnesses who attested to his presence. Some of the police officers themselves had seen him arrive home and pull into his driveway. To account for the time difference between his departure from the bar and arrival at home, Michael told White that he had stopped at a park and taken a walk. He was naturally depressed about his job situation and walking helped with his anxiety. This was of course a lie, but Michael hoped it would be enough to sway some jurors toward reasonable doubt.

Through the discovery process White learned that the State had a witness who had seen Michael enter the home of Max and Connor. The witness was old man Gallagher. Michael suggested that the old man's memory was off and he was thinking of another day when Michael had gone to speak with Connor about Max's behavior. He also questioned Gallagher's vision. They had also found two hair follicles in Max's blood and the DNA was a match to Michael. He confronted Michael with this and told him that if he didn't come clean with his attorney, he would have to find another one. Michael assured him that he was telling the truth. He didn't understand the hair being there except that he was a neighbor and had been in Connor's house many times.

They went into the trial with this strategy and Michael and Amanda could only hope that it would be enough to at least plant doubt in the minds of some jurors. The first prosecution witness was Connor, who told how Michael and Amanda were always accusing Max of hurting their son Johnny. Max always denied this and Connor had no reason to doubt his son. Max was always truthful with him. He then relayed that Michael had threatened that if the abuse didn't stop, there would be a price to pay and he and Max would be paying it.

Next old man Gallagher testified that he saw Michael knock on the front door and then go inside the house. He was sure about the date because he was getting groceries from his car when he saw this and they always bought groceries on Thursday. He had a receipt to prove it. He also testified that he had excellent vision when wearing his glasses which he had on that day. A neighbor whose backyard faced the backdoor of Connor's house said that he was outside raking leaves when he saw a man come out of the backdoor. He said that the man was not Connor but he didn't get a good look at his face and was distracted by a phone call and returned to his house before seeing what the man did. He didn't actually see him crash through the door. A forensic scientist testified that the hair follicles found in Max's blood was a DNA match to Michael. A psychiatrist testified next saying it was most likely that Michael was seething with anger when he went there and would have easily flown into a rage. He might not have gone there intending bodily harm but the least little thing would have ignited his anger. The multiple stab wounds were evidence of this rage in his professional opinion.

The prosecution ended its case by calling a surprise witness. The defense argued strenuously against this as they had not been notified, but the Assistant D.A. said that they had just uncovered this witness and had not had time to follow the normal procedures for notifying the defense. The judge allowed the witness who turned out to be the person from the city landfill where Michael had taken the bag of bloody clothes. He testified that he distinctly and positively remembered a man showing up with a bag of trash on the day of murder and was confident that Michael was that man. He said he remembered it well because he was preparing to shut down the entrance to the landfill for the day when Michael pulled up at the last minute. His son had a birthday party that evening and he was annoyed that this person had arrived so late and would probably cause him to be late to the party.

Connor and Amanda also testified about the relationship between the boys. Connor painted a much more congenial friendship, while Amanda told of the continuous cases of bullying. Although Michael thought Amanda was much more convincing, it was really a case of he said, she said. Who would the jury believe?

In the end the jury was out for six hours and returned a verdict of guilty of second degree murder. They found him not guilty of burglary. Various witnesses for and against Michael testified in the sentencing phase. Connor showed more emotion than either Michael or Amanda had ever seen from him. With tears rolling down his cheeks he told of losing his wife and now his son. He cast Michael as a controlling parent who was always accusing Max of things that simply were not true.

The judge addressed Michael and told him that killing a 12-year old child is abhorrent and reprehensible. He had in his twenty plus years on the bench seen very few cases as disturbing as this one. He could not imagine a situation that was so bad that it should end the way this dispute had ended. He also said that he could not set any precedent for mercy in a case like this. He then sentenced Michael to the maximum penalty of twenty years for his crime. He would be eligible for parole in twelve years.

Michael had feared, but somehow expected the verdict from the early days of the investigation and trial. He now turned toward Amanda and the officer allowed her and Johnny to hug him. He then began the walk to his cell, to his destiny for the next twelve to twenty years. His only consolation was that he had saved Amanda from this fate and he knew she would raise Johnny well. He had protected his family.

CHAPTER NINE

To say that prison life was a totally new experience would be the epitome of understatement. But given enough time everything develops into a routine of sorts and prison had a very definite routine. Michael had been there for a little over two months now and had settled into that routine. Everyone awoke at the crack of dawn every morning for breakfast and then they were deployed to their assigned jobs and activities. Michael had been selected for duty in the laundry room and spent most of his day there with a break for lunch. His duties normally ended about 3:00 every afternoon. He then had an hour of free time in the main prison yard and another hour in his cell where he read a book from the library before going to dinner at 5:00. In the evenings he would either be allowed to watch television with other inmates or he would return to his cell. The next day would be a repeat of the previous one except for Saturday when the laundry was closed and he was afforded more television and yard time. Then on Sunday he attended chapel services in the morning and a bible study that afternoon. He couldn't say it was a bad life except for not seeing Amanda and Johnny every day, and it was as satisfying as sitting in the Dugout Sports Bar and Grill had been.

Amanda would visit him every Saturday. She would normally arrive around 2:00 PM and stay for an hour or so. She would bring him up to date on Johnny's activities in school and on his baseball team. She said that it was really hard on Johnny at first and some kids teased him at school, but he had told them that his Dad was a hero for saving him from a bully and shouldn't even be in prison. She was proud of how well he had handled the teasing and how well he was adjusting. They also discussed her work and of course he told her of his routine in the prison. She kept him informed about the house and financial matters. Since she had been their sole bread winner for several months, their finances had really not suffered with him gone away.

Johnny would normally not come with her. He didn't like seeing his dad in this place. But he would usually accompany her on the first Saturday of each month. It always thrilled and uplifted Michael to see him.

There was always talk about the appeals process also. The attorney was exploring different options for making an appeal, but neither she nor Michael held out any real hope for this to come to anything. The trial had been conducted fairly; there was no known reason to question any of the jurors. The only unusual thing was the surprise witness but that just didn't seem to be enough to raise any false hope. Michael was pretty sure he was in for at least twelve years.

His fellow inmates were a mixed lot. As he got to know more about them, he learned that several were career criminals as you might expect and were here for the second, third, or even fourth time. They were comprised of murderers like himself, rapists, burglars, people guilty of assault and battery, and numerous other crimes. As he studied the different personalities he determined that a large majority of his new neighbors fell into one of two categories. The first were those who, like Max, were bullies. They had used unnecessary force and bullied others for their entire lives. That was their modus operandi. They had been bullies for so long that they knew no other way. He hadn't seen enough to say this with certainty but his belief was that the chance of reform for any of these men was next to zero. There might be the occasional transformation or religious conversion that really resulted in change, but they were by far the exception and not the rule.

The second category was those that had been bullied most of their lives. Many of these had taken all they could from parents, partners, so-called friends and then finally lashed out at their abusers. He could definitely identify with this group, but he also could see where his own son might have ended up this way eventually if Amanda hadn't stepped in and did what she did. If he had to serve time to pay for that, then so be it. In the long run it was probably worth it for Johnny's sake.

Another thing that he had learned in these first few months was that he had to be very careful talking about his own reason for being imprisoned. Child abusers were considered the worst type of scum by his fellow inmates. Many of them from each of the two camps had been victims of child abuse, often by their own parents, and blamed it for their being here. It had scarred them physically and emotionally and helped mold them into the criminals that they were. If they identified Michael as an abuser, many of them would not hesitate to take out their own form of revenge on him. So he kept quiet as much as possible about the details of his crime, but no matter how circumspect you are the news always gets out and so he tried to watch his back at all times. He hoped that as his time here grew they would see that he wasn't really that kind of person and the threat level would go down.

Unfortunately that time never came. One Saturday morning he was out in the yard with the other prisoners. He seldom joined them in any of their games, but he often would watch as they played basketball, volleyball, or other sports. Today he was watching them play basketball when the whistle blew for everyone to return to the cells. It was nearing time for lunch. He didn't notice that as he walked towards the building a group of guys crowded around him. Actually this wasn't even unusual since they were all returning at the same time. Then one of the men in front of him suddenly spun around and faced him. The man lunged with his right hand and Michael felt a sharp burning in his chest. The man turned back around and proceeded toward the building and those behind him passed by as he crumpled to the ground. The guards finally saw him and sounded an alarm. They summoned the medics, but it was too late. By the time they got him to the infirmary Michael was dead. They never found the inmate or the shiv he had used to kill Michael.

Lying on the green grass of the yard, Michael thought back on his life. No, your whole life doesn't pass by you in those final minutes but you do think about the important things. He knew that he had been blessed. Growing up he had loving parents who would do anything for him. He had met a wonderful woman who loved him. Amanda was the best thing that ever happened to him. Oh, they had grown a little apart lately but he knew that if he had gotten a job things would have returned to normal. They would have been okay. And Johnny was a great kid. He knew that he would grow up to be an outstanding man. And he knew that he had done what he had to do to protect the two of them. He had no regrets as his thoughts faded and he took his last breath.

CHAPTER TEN

Amanda was absolutely beaming as she returned from the prison infirmary. It had not been her plan that Michael would die in prison, but now that it had happened she viewed it as the best possible outcome. She had toyed with this idea for quite some time as Johnny suffered at the hands of Max. If she could somehow eliminate Max and see that Michael was blamed for it, then she would be rid of a bully and a deadbeat husband. Toying with the idea was one thing but actually carrying it out was quite another. She had never really thought that it would happen until that fateful day when she killed Max. She had indeed gone over there consumed with anger and had intended to somehow bring this problem to an end. But when she wrestled that knife from Max's hand in the kitchen everything had changed. She had gone into a rage unlike anything she had ever experienced and at the end of it, Max was dead. She panicked at first but then as she calmed down she realized that this was her chance to do just what she had dreamed of doing. So she called Michael and pulled him into the situation.

Michael had done just as she expected he would. He had taken control and cleaned up the scene in the kitchen. Then he had taken her bag of bloody clothes to the landfill to get rid of them. It was after he left the house to go to the landfill that she ran to the bathroom and found some hairs embedded in his comb. She knew that Connor would arrive home at any moment so she ran quickly to his house and planted the hairs in the blood next to the knife that Michael had wiped clean. Then she retreated to her own house and prayed that no one had seen her enter the other home.

Next she started looking at attorneys, anticipating that Michael would eventually be arrested. She knew someone might have seen her enter earlier also but she hoped that the hairs and Michael's previous encounter with Connor and Max would point more to him than her. She found Benjamin White who was a relatively young and inexperienced attorney. He did, as she told Michael, have excellent reviews but they were mostly for civil cases. His criminal experience seemed limited. Then, being cautiously prepared, she found another more seasoned attorney who she would call if they arrested her instead. She also could recommend him if Michael researched White and objected to using him. But as usual, Michael had fully trusted her judgement. She regretted having to use part of her 401(k) for bail money, but she accepted that as part of the price for her freedom.

The truth was she had known for some time now that Michael had given up on finding a new job. She understood the depression at first and assumed that it would pass and he would renew his search for employment. Not being as technically proficient as Amanda, he had probably forgotten that she could track his location on her cell phone. She knew that all his supposed interviews and meetings with employment agencies were in fact just time spent at the Dugout Sports Bar and Grill. That was bad, but what made things even worse was that the love had gone out of their marriage. Over the past two years their passion had died and they lived more like two strangers sharing a room than a married couple. They had kept up appearances for Johnny's sake, but they both knew that things were different between them.

Her plan of course had not been for Michael to die. She couldn't do that to Johnny who adored his father. No, she had simply planned to wait an appropriate time, around two years, and then quietly seek a divorce. But now that tragedy had struck she realized that it was the best of all worlds. There would be no divorce, no property to settle, no need for Johnny to visit his dad in prison. This was much cleaner.

Of course she would play the grieving widow. She would continue to tell Johnny that his dad was a hero who should never have gone to prison and certainly should never have died there. Johnny would grieve for a while. He would miss his dad, as he already did. But kids were so resilient. In the long run he would be okay and she knew she could provide everything he needed including love and support.

Now came the hard part. He had gone to baseball practice and planned to spend the night with one of his friends. She would go and pick him up and break this horrible news to him. She would put on her saddest face. She would cry. Her voice would tremble. She would comfort her son who would be doing his own crying. They would get through this together. They would be strong.

She now stared into the mirror in her bedroom and prepared herself mentally for this performance. Then suddenly she smiled and her face lit up again. She was in control of herself and knew she could do it. But until she picked Johnny up, she could enjoy this moment. She had done everything she had hoped to do and life was good.

The Perfect Plan

by
Bobby J Watson

The enemy of a good plan
is the dream of a perfect plan.

-Carl Von Clausewitz

CHAPTER ONE

Roger Carlson was a man to be envied. He was the Chief Accountant for a billion dollar conglomerate that owned numerous successful subsidiaries. He reported directly to the Chief Financial Officer and would undoubtedly be considered for that position when the current title holder retired. He owned a large two story home in an upscale neighborhood of the city and he drove to work each day in a smart looking BMW, while his beautiful wife drove around town in a spiffy new Corvette. He had two good looking children who were just entering adulthood, a boy and a girl, who had gone to the city's most prestigious private academy and were now in college. Yes, Roger Carlson was a man to be envied and yet he was miserable.

He hated his wife. Oh sure, at one time he had thought he was the luckiest man on earth. Darcy was a strikingly beautiful woman who even as she approached fifty made men turn their heads and stare at her as she walked by. They had started dating during their freshman year in college. Roger was a running back on the freshman football team and went to the school on a full scholarship. He wasn't a bad looking guy and had his pick of girls who threw themselves at guys on the team. Darcy however was different. She knew that she was attractive and had no need to throw herself at anyone. The guys all came sniffing around her door and Roger was the lucky one she settled upon. They became engaged four years later after graduating and got married six months after that.

Darcy had a marketing degree and went to work for a national retailer while Roger hooked on with the billion dollar conglomerate. The company was smaller then but had grown steadily during his twenty-five year tenure and he had advanced with it, starting as an accounting intern and now leading the entire staff. As he grew more successful, Darcy became more restless. She was really more intent on being involved in the society circles than in advancing her career. After five years they agreed that she could become a stay-at-home mom while Roger took on the role of sole breadwinner. She almost immediately hired a maid who watched the house and the kids while she worked at becoming a starlet in high society. There were numerous events, country club memberships, and activities to which she devoted herself. Of course to really be successful she had to have the best clothes, and fashion requires constant updating. To achieve her goals she also needed an impressive house and car. These outward signs of success were critical to her mission. Instead of the sweet wife she had once been, she became a constant nag needing more and more and more. Roger grudgingly went along with all of this and attended formal balls and other events as required. But even as his career advanced he struggled to meet her increasingly lavish demands. As Darcy reached the pinnacle she so desired, Roger became more miserable every day.

His daughter Jillian had apparently been a close observer of her mother and was just as demanding. When she turned sixteen she had to have a car and not just any car, but a sporty little convertible that cost a small fortune. She explained to Roger that she deserved this because her older brother had a nice vehicle. Her clothing needs rivaled her mother also. It seemed to Roger that teenage fashion changed almost every day and keeping up with it was nearly impossible. And for being a good dad and supplying all of these things, did Roger receive any gratitude or thanks? No, mostly he got ignored because almost every minute she was at home was spent on her cell phone. TikTok, Instagram, videos, chats and texting was her full-time job it seemed. If he tried to engage her in conversation or suggest they do something fun together, he got a look that was both condescending and scalding. The only time that look changed was when she wanted more. Good old dad was just an ATM. Now in college, she had been accepted into a sorority populated by rich girls and each was intent on trying to outdo the other. Apparently study was low on the list of requirements as she struggled to avoid flunking out of school every semester.

Evan was a year older than Jillian. When he was a little boy he and Roger had been very close. Every time Roger left the house, Evan wanted to tag along with his dad. They had been constant companions when Roger was at home. They did all the things that father and son were supposed to do together. They had eaten ice cream cones, played pitch in the backyard, gone hiking, camping and fishing. Almost every Saturday they had gone to the movies to watch an animated flick or a good action movie featuring a super-hero. Things had changed when Evan turned about thirteen or fourteen. Those are often difficult years when growing up and Evan started hanging out more with friends from school. Dad slowly became more of an embarrassment than a pal. Some of his friends turned out to be the wrong kind of friends and he was arrested for shoplifting. Roger reasoned it was a one-time mistake and Evan seemed pretty shaken up by it but that didn't last long. When he was sixteen Roger had bought him a new car and thought this might bring them closer together again. Instead Evan disappeared most of the time. His friends had introduced him to drinking and recreational drugs and his resentment for his dad had grown. Like Jillian he had enrolled in college, but it only lasted one semester. He now wanted nothing to do with Roger or any of the family and seemed headed for trouble. It was just a matter of time.

Roger entered the corporate office building and got on the elevator. It was packed and several people spoke to him respectfully as Mr. Carlson. Exiting on the top floor he saw the

CFO and the current CEO speaking in the hallway and both stopped and greeted him and shook his hand. He entered his office area and was met by Valerie Blanchard, his Assistant. Valerie was in her mid-thirties and was an excellent accountant in her own right. She had been with the company and had worked with Roger for almost ten years now and Roger had complete confidence in her. She in turn looked up to him and admired his ability and the position he had attained in the company.

Yes, Roger Carlson was a man to be envied but he hated his wife, he hated his kids, he hated his family. He thought about divorce but in this state the alimony alone would kill him. Let's be honest. He had even dreamed of ways to kill the lot of them and start afresh, but Roger was no murderer. He was however a long-term planner of the utmost ability.

CHAPTER TWO

Five years ago Roger had decided that enough was enough. He sat in his office now drinking a morning cup of coffee and reflecting on that decision. He deserved to spend the second half of his life in pleasant surroundings doing the things that he loved. He really didn't care what happened to his family. He had given them plenty and the time had come when they could learn to get by on their own. He could just imagine the fit, the conniption that Darcy would throw when she found out that he had deserted her. Her place with the high society hoity-toities would come crashing down. She might even have to get a job and work for a living. What a shame! She wouldn't be able to afford the house and would probably be forced to sell the Corvette. He couldn't help but smirk as he thought about the plight she would face.

Jillian would have to leave school if she hadn't already flunked out by the time he actually disappeared. The tuition at the private university was too high and there was no way she would merit a scholarship. She would learn that the loyalty of her sorority sisters ran only so deep. She would also come to the frightening understanding that very few people can earn a living on their cell phones as social influencers. He could not imagine a job for which she would be qualified. Perhaps a wait person or hostess at a diner or restaurant. Who knows, some honest work like that might make her a better person.

He had no doubt how Evan would make out. Whether it was a car thief, a burglar, or a dope dealer Evan would end up in prison. He didn't like to think about this but he was also convinced that his staying around would not alter the direction of Evan's life. He was beyond Roger's ability to help. While this made him sad, it did not make him feel a bit guilty about his plan to disappear and start a new life. He had done all he could, maybe he had failed as a father but he had done all he could and he was determined to find happiness in the remainder of his own life.

Roger was a brilliant and creative accountant. He was also a very good long-term planner and most importantly he was a very patient man. When he invested in stocks or mutual funds he didn't nervously check the market every day and he never panicked just because a stock had a selloff. He had done his research and knew that his investments were in sound companies that would do well in the long run. He was patient and he exercised that same patience with his plan.

He had first devised his plan five years earlier. Even then he could see the future and knew that he wanted a fresh start in life. He had played an integral part in choosing the financial software that was used by the home office and every subsidiary. He had been one of the leaders most involved in setting up that system. He had created the Chart of Accounts that was the basis for each company and he had a detailed knowledge of the daily workings of each one. Implementing that system in each company had been a two-year project but he walked away from it knowing more about it than anyone else.

He had started small and slowly grown his scheme over those years. He created fraudulent vendors and accounts that paid small yet reasonable amounts to various shell companies that he had created. He knew the personnel at each subsidiary and the type of payments that would look legitimate for that business. He also knew the employees who would easily overlook these payments and the ones who were more competent and might question them. These he avoided.

Each year he added a few more payments and as the company added new subsidiaries he planted fraudulent accounts with them also after observing the strengths and weaknesses of the staff. The shell companies that he created all appeared to have legitimate ties to the subsidiaries that paid them for services. Unknown to anyone but himself all of these shell companies had one thing in common. They all used the same bank account and on a routine basis he transferred money from that account to an offshore account.

Like any large corporation his company had their books audited annually by a major accounting firm. The first year after initiating his plan he was a nervous wreck when the audit occurred. He convinced himself that despite his careful planning and execution, these auditors would find something that he had overlooked. After all they were professionals, the best of the best. Why did he think he could fool them?

The audit took three weeks and he was on pins and needles the entire time. He had no appetite and he barely slept at night. Whenever they came to his office to ask questions he felt his stomach churn and his heart sink. He was sure they were on to him. But no, in the end they found nothing and the company passed the audit with flying colors. The second year he was almost as nervous as the first but once again they found nothing of concern. Since then he had grown more confident that his plan would work. There was no reason that it would not. It was the perfect plan.

But now the time had come for the next step in that plan. It was time to make his move and disappear. It was the right time for a number of reasons. Number one was simply not pressing his luck. No matter how perfect the plan, someone would stumble on to it eventually. Number two he had all he could take of his ungrateful family. He simply couldn't stand being with them any longer. Number three and most important was that if he wanted to enjoy the second half of his life, the time had come to start that journey.

Just like with the first part of the plan, he had also planned this one well and knew exactly what to do next. Now was the time to finalize it.

CHAPTER THREE

The planning for this next step had begun years ago at the same time the first step was hatched. The first decision Roger had to make was where to live once he cashed in his riches. There were several countries that had no formal extradition treaties with the United States but that did not guarantee they would not extradite a criminal. A criminal? He didn't think of himself in those terms but legally he knew that was exactly what he was. He easily crossed some countries off his list without giving them much thought. We might not be at war with Vietnam any more but that didn't mean he wanted to live there. Botswana, Uganda, Cambodia were eliminated just as quickly. Qatar was somewhat appealing but research showed that they do a pretty thorough background check, especially if you're coming from the US. Besides that, he didn't relish the idea of living in the Middle East. That part of the world presented too many problems.

One country that had seemed appealing was the tiny country of Montenegro. It was a tiny country in southeast Europe not far from Greece and it had a nice coastal area. The big drawback there was that English was not a prevalent language. Instead most people spoke the native tongue or Bosnian or Serbian and he had no confidence he could master any of those. Another country that held even greater interest was The Maldives. These islands seemed quite appealing with beautiful beaches and fishing opportunities. There were some limitations to lifestyle because of the Islamic beliefs, such as no pork and very limited alcohol but these weren't that big a drawback. Roger enjoyed the occasional drink but he was not a heavy drinker. The Maldives were indeed a close second but he had finally settled on the island nation of Vanuatu.

Vanuatu was near Australia and the official languages were English and French. Roger had taken French in college and assumed that he could recall and learn enough to carry on a basic conversation when necessary. Like The Maldives it had wonderful beaches and was a scuba divers paradise with coral reefs and an old shipwreck that drew a lot of attention from diving enthusiasts. He had done a little scuba diving and looked forward to becoming more practiced at it. Property ownership in Vanuatu was also a possibility if he decided to buy a home or invest in property. Tourism was on the rise and offered a lot of possibilities for such investment. Perhaps most important however were two things. First they had no extradition treaty with the United States and secondly you could purchase legal citizenship for $150,000. The protections of citizenship could prove invaluable if he was ever found by the FBI or other agencies.

Even before he had settled on a location, he had set about a different task. He had researched this and now took the step of entering the world of the dark web and searching for a fake identification. Just as with the research on various countries, he did this on his personal laptop so there would be no record of it on the corporate network. They make getting a fake ID look easy on television, but it's not that simple. But after doing due diligence, he was able to obtain a fraudulent birth certificate, driver license and passport. The new documents actually arrived via FedEx and as he examined them he was impressed with their seeming authenticity. This had without doubt been the scariest part of the entire plan. His first use of the new identification was to create an offshore bank account in the Cayman Islands.

So as he sat in his office that morning and reflected on his past preparations, he logged into the corporate system and put in a request for one week of vacation starting the following week. He would tell Darcy that he had to make a business trip that week. He attended two or three conferences a year so she would suspect nothing unusual. At lunch that same day he went to a nearby travel agency and booked a round trip flight, hotel and rental car for Vanuatu. Although he had read about the island nation, he had never actually been there. Another good thing about this island was that they drove on the right side of the road so he wouldn't have to adapt to driving differently. He broke the news to Darcy that evening. She seemed to think nothing of it. He had made all of these travel plans using his fake identification. It was his first time to use these credentials for international travel. William Tyson would be the one making the trip.

Leaving early the next Monday he drove to LAX International Airport and checked in for his flight. He sweated bullets and his stomach ached as he approached the ticket counter and got his boarding pass, but the agent accepted his credentials without any concern. The security officer at the international terminal examined his passport and boarding pass and seemed to look at him for quite some time. But maybe that was just his imagination. Finally the officer passed the wand over his body because he had forgotten to take the keys out of his pocket. Roger was so nervous by now that he thought he might throw up, but he struggled to look cool, calm and collected. He breathed a huge sigh of relief as he dashed to his gate.

Roger flew Fiji Airlines from Los Angeles to the capital of Port Vila, a city of just over 50,000 where he rented a car and drove to a popular resort hotel near the beach. The flight had taken just over twenty hours so he immediately hit the bed and went to sleep but not before setting his alarm for the next morning. The next day he explored the main island and a couple of others and fell in love with the beauty of the beaches and surrounding areas. The rest of the week was spent looking at homes for purchase and condos for long-term rent. He would have to decide whether he wanted to purchase or not, but either way he knew he could live like a king here. But he also knew he would not overdo it and be too extravagant. One thing he did not want to do was draw too much attention to himself. After house hunting, he actually spent a day doing some snorkling and deep sea fishing. The last day before departing he checked on the citizenship requirements at a government office and assured himself that for the requisite cash he could easily and quickly become a citizen.

The return flight was somewhat shorter, only taking fourteen hours the majority of which he spent sleeping. He arrived home and Darcy seemed happy to see him. She noted that he must have gotten some sun on his trip as he seemed a bit more tan than he had before. He smiled to himself and thought *if only she knew*.

CHAPTER FOUR

Roger never gave the office a thought while on his excursion to Vanuatu and back. One reason of course was that he didn't plan to be employed much longer. The other reason was that he had complete faith in the ability of his assistant, Valerie Blanchard. Technically he had left Roland Charles in command as the acting Chief Accountant but Valerie was the one who really kept things going smoothly and Roland would depend on her just as much as Roger did. Valerie had been with the company for ten years and, while her title officially was Assistant to the Chief Accountant, she was much more than a typical Admin. She was a top-notch accountant, a CPA, and she knew the internal workings of the company almost as well as Roger himself.

Valerie was a diligent worker and also a pleasant person that everyone liked but few knew her that well. She was single and seemed to be dedicated to nothing but her job. She shared very little about her personal life and while everyone liked and admired her place in the company, they almost universally viewed her as essentially an old maid. Well, she wasn't really that old. She was in her mid-thirties and was a fairly attractive woman. She in turn looked up to Roger. She admired his skill as an accountant and his own rise within the company. She wasn't without ambition herself and hoped to be in the running for his job, or at least that of Roland Charles, when Roger stepped up to the position of Chief Financial Officer.

Valerie had great respect for Roger's privacy and only entered his office when absolutely necessary during his absence, but Roland had asked for some reports that were kept in Roger's office and she entered it to retrieve them on Tuesday during Roger's vacation week. His decision to take vacation had caught her somewhat by surprise. He usually planned things months in advance and advised her of his plans, and this had seemed like a spur of the moment decision. Oh well, she guessed he was entitled to the time off and maybe the trip was simply an opportunity that had arisen unexpectedly.

She knew he kept these reports in a cabinet behind his desk and opened a door to look for them. While rifling through some papers trying to find the reports she saw a sheet of paper that looked somewhat like a bank statement and the description of the account did not look at all familiar. The account totaled a little over seven and a half million dollars and it really puzzled her. She knew the accounts inside and out but this one was a complete mystery. After studying it for a few moments she continued searching and found the reports that Roland had requested and took them to him. But she couldn't get that bank statement out of her mind.

After everyone else had left for the day she went back to Roger's office and looked again at that statement. She then ran a report that listed all of the bank accounts for the company and its subsidiaries. As she suspected this account was not one of them. She knew that Roger had a nice salary but there was no way he would have this much in his personal account. She also knew this was not a 401(k) or brokerage statement. The account actually had a company name and it didn't ring a bell either. She left the office and headed to her apartment, just as mystified as she had been when she first stumbled onto the statement.

The next morning she sat down at her cubicle outside of Roger's office and still couldn't get that bank statement out of her mind. She knew that Roger was not involved in any other business or even charities where he would be managing a bank account. Finally she had a thought and kept going back and forth trying to decide whether or not to pursue it. The company required almost every vendor to complete an electronic ACH Authorization Form that enabled the company to pay them by direct deposit. This was much faster and easier than the old school method of writing checks. She decided to pursue her idea and ran a query of every vendor along with their bank routing code and account number. It was a huge, lengthy list. She then sorted the information by those same two numbers and looked for duplicates. Then finding the mystery account number in the list she found that there were fourteen different vendors who had their payments deposited to this same account. That certainly seemed odd and as she then investigated those vendors it became even more so.

These vendors were spread out among the main company and various subsidiaries and by their description and other data seemed to have nothing that would tie them together. She didn't want to think that Roger was doing something illegal but this was certainly very unusual to say the least. She then started researching the company name on the bank account and could find precious little about it. It was registered as a corporation and that was about it. It had all the markings of a shell company. To make matters more suspicious the vendor companies depositing into the account looked like shell companies as well. There was simply no detail information to be found about these businesses. She didn't want to raise an alarm yet but she did discretely call the Payables Clerks for a couple of her subsidiaries and they really knew nothing about these vendors either. Their invoices were generally small amounts and they just paid them by the due dates.

Valerie was torn. She didn't want to accuse Roger of anything and yet this all seemed too strange to be above board. She needed to learn more about the bank account and the company but she had pretty much exhausted her resources. She did however know someone who could probably dig deeper, but was she ready to take that step? Once taken there might be no return.

CHAPTER FIVE

Valerie went home to her apartment that evening and poured herself a full glass of red wine. She had never felt so torn in her life. Roger had always been very good to her and had encouraged her in her career more than anyone else. He had chosen her as his assistant because he believed in her. She desperately wanted to be loyal to him. She told herself that she really didn't know enough to accuse him of anything. But she also knew that what she had found defied any logical explanation. It had all the markings of fraud, specifically embezzlement. She drank her wine and sat motionless on her sofa. She was transfixed in thought and didn't even hear her boyfriend when he entered the apartment.

"You look beat" he said as he sat down by her. While most people at work may have thought she was a loner who was totally devoted to her job and nothing else, she had actually been in a relationship for several years now. She and her boyfriend Alex Stroud shared the apartment and they were officially engaged although they had no wedding date and felt no urgency to set one.

"It was a busy day at work, what with Roger gone and Roland in charge" she told him.

"You were really out of it when I came in. You didn't even hear me. Is something really big or bad going on at the office"?

Alex was just short of six feet tall and started most of his days at the gym. He had short-cut brown hair and eyes to match. He was two years younger than Valerie and he was also an FBI field agent. He primarily investigated financial crimes involving interstate commerce and if there was anyone who could find more information for her, it was Alex. But she couldn't bring herself to divulge the real reason for her concern.

"No, not really. Just preparing for month-end close and all the reporting that goes with it. Roger always knows just what to do, but Roland has needed quite a bit of help." There was a modicum of truth to this but it wasn't really what was on her mind.

"Well, how about I take you out to dinner then and get your mind off of it" he offered. "Another glass of wine or two and a nice steak and I think you'll be fine."

"That does sound like the right medicine" she replied, trying to sound upbeat.

It was a nice dinner and it actually did help soothe her mind at least temporarily. After dinner they returned to the apartment and snuggled on the sofa as they watched a movie. She fell asleep and missed the ending as her head rested comfortably on Alex's shoulder.

The next day was Thursday and as she drove to work her anxiety rose with each block nearer to the office. Any relief that Alex had given her the night before was gone by the time she pulled into the parking garage. Once at her desk she addressed some items that needed to be taken care of but her mind was simply not on the tasks as she performed them. She found herself drinking more coffee than normal, and the caffeine only added to her anxiety.

Finally she tried once again to search the internet and see if she could find any information about these shell companies. Whoever had set them up had definitely known what they were doing. She discovered a few supposed officer names for the companies but then could find nothing helpful about these people. They were either fictitious or simply names that had been used specifically because they had no business profile.

She went home that night more exhausted than she had been the previous night. Tomorrow was Friday and Roger would be back next week. What would she do? Should she ask him about these companies and the bank statement? Should she act as if all was normal and nothing was wrong? These thoughts kept running through her mind as she drove home. This time when she entered the apartment Alex had beat her home and he immediately knew that something was really upsetting her. Maybe he was just intuitive or maybe it was part of his training but he had no doubt that this was not the Valerie he knew and loved.

"Okay, Val" he said. "Enough is enough. This is more than just normal work stress. What is going on? And no evading the question this time."

"Oh, God Alex. You're right and I just don't know what to do."

"Well sit down here and tell ole Alex all about it and maybe I can help."

She explained to Alex what she had found. He asked her to make a picture of the bank statement and send it to him the next morning. He would see what he could find out about the account and the company. Alex had a great deal of experience and he also had the resources of the FBI behind him.

"I just hate the thought of getting Roger into trouble, and what if I throw all this suspicion on him and it turns out to be something with a perfectly reasonable explanation? I've just been sick this week worrying about all of this."

"Yes honey, I know that you have. I knew something was wrong and I understand your feelings towards Roger. He's really helped you move up the ladder with him. I know that and here's what I will do. I shouldn't even say this. I could get fired in a heartbeat if anyone even heard me say this. But I'll find out what I can and keep it as quiet as I can. Then I'll tell you everything and you can decide if you want to report it to the executives at the company or not. If you decide not to pursue it then neither of us knows anything about it. Does that sound agreeable to you?"

"Yes, I think so and I would never do anything to get you in trouble with the bureau. I just hope it turns out to be nothing."

With that she prepared them a light meal that they enjoyed while watching another movie on TV. She again fell asleep with her head on his shoulder. All the while she was fearing the worst and hoping for the best.

CHAPTER SIX

Valerie arrived early at the office the next day. It was now Friday and Roger would be back at work the following Monday. She went into his office before other employees started coming in and took a picture of the bank statement with her phone. She sent the picture to Alex as he had requested and he responded with a "thumbs up" emoji indicating he had received it.

She went about her normal activities for the rest of the day. She and Roland worked on several reports and minor tasks in preparation for Roger's return. At one point she smiled to herself and thought *this is the most normal day I've had since Monday, before I found that stupid statement.*

That evening she and Alex went out to dinner again. It had become part of their normal routine to dine out on Friday nights. They went to an Italian restaurant that they both enjoyed. After having a cocktail and appetizers Alex ordered Shrimp Alfredo which was one of his favorites. Valerie in turn ordered Eggplant Parmigiana which was one of her most frequent choices. They then both topped off the meal with cheesecake for dessert.

As they waited for their cheesecake she couldn't wait any longer and asked, "Okay mister, what's the verdict? What did you find out?"

"Well I want to work on it some more this weekend and I will need a little more help from you but I think that your boss is in big trouble."

Her heart sank in her chest. "How big?"

"Well the seven and half million you found in that account is just a fraction of what's been deposited. Over the last few years there have been transfers about every six months from that account to an offshore account and the total is in the neighborhood of eighty-two million dollars."

"Oh my God, Alex! You've got to be kidding. Are all the deposits from our company?"

"Every single one that I found came from an ACH payment from your company."

"So, it really does look like Roger is stealing it" she stated in a low and disappointed voice.

"It seems that way but I want to do more digging and I want you to get some more information next week. I'll go into the details later this weekend."

"Okay, but he's back on Monday so I'll have to be really careful."

"I understand. But let's try not to worry about it now. It's a federal crime to worry when you're eating cheesecake" he said as their dessert arrived.

They enjoyed the rest of their dinner and then decided to go see a movie at a local theatre. It was a silly romantic comedy and they watched and laughed as they munched on buttered popcorn. It was nice to do something relaxing and fun for a change and a strange calmness started coming over Valerie as she watched the movie. She reasoned that she had done nothing wrong and if Roger was indeed guilty and got caught that was the risk he had assumed. It wasn't on her.

The next day Alex got up early and went deep sea fishing with another couple of agents. The three of them loved fishing in the ocean and had gone in together to purchase a large ocean fishing boat. It was far from a yacht but it enabled them to pursue the sport they enjoyed. They didn't always go out together. More often one of them would notify the other two and use the boat on their own, but today the trio was on the high seas together. Alex came home with a nice sea bass that he had dressed on the boat and broiled it for dinner. It was delicious and he and Valerie declared that it was every bit as good as the Italian food the night before.

As they enjoyed the sea bass he told her what he needed her to do next.

"I want you to get a list of invoices from the vendors using that bank account. Get a list that includes at least this year and further back if you can."

"Okay, that shouldn't be too difficult" she answered.

"The other stuff may be harder" he said. "I want you to look for any information you can find that might be a user id or password for an offshore bank account. The bank is in the Cayman Islands and I have the account number but they won't divulge anything without us getting warrants and maybe not even then. If you can get us the information to get into the account, then that would be easier and helps us keep this quiet until we know the whole story."

"I do have his password for both his company PC and his personal laptop. That may help but there's no guarantee I can find a user id and password. "

"I know but he may keep them in a Word Document or something. You'd be surprised how many people do that. And the other thing is I want you to search his office and see if you can see any evidence of his having gotten a false id. Odds are that he has one and used it to open that offshore account."

"Oh lord. You're asking for a lot of digging. Tomorrow is Sunday. I think I'll go in while the office is empty and see what I can find."

"Yeah that's probably a good idea. I'm going to see if I can uncover anything else on that account tomorrow, but I'm not too hopeful that I'll find anything useful."

"I'll have to stay late after everyone leaves on Monday to search his personal laptop. He took that with him on vacation."

"Makes sense. I know this is asking a lot of you Val but it's our best chance of finding out what's going on and keeping it quiet."

"I know. I'll do the best I can. Wish me luck."

"Always."

CHAPTER SEVEN

Valerie went to the office as planned on Sunday morning. She made herself a cup of coffee using the Keurig machine. She wanted to switch to decaffeinated but today she felt like she could use the caffeine. Sitting and sipping on the hot brew she wondered why she had ever taken notice of that bank statement. What a can of worms it had turned out to be. And honestly while it was theft, her company was so huge it wouldn't really miss eight-two million over a number of years. Oh well, she couldn't just forget about it now. She had to move forward.

Running a report on the fourteen subsidiaries was not that difficult but all those invoices created a large number of pages. She managed to go back three years which should give Alex all the detail he could ever need. Rather than print the four hundred plus pages, she emailed the pdf file to her personal email address and then deleted the report and the email from the sent folder of her PC. She smiled to herself and thought that Alex could print the report at the FBI's expense.

She then went into Roger's office and logged into his PC. There had been occasions over the years when he was absent from the office, found he needed something and had asked her to access his PC. Thus she had known his password for quite a while now and even though the IT Department recommended everyone change their passwords ever so many months, hardly anyone ever seemed to follow that advice. Once logged in she made an extensive search of all his folders and Word files and found no evidence of a user id, password or fake identification. That didn't really surprise her. If he stored information like that it would more likely be on his personal computer. Fortunately for her he changed that password as often as the one on his company PC.

She then returned home to their apartment and sent Alex the report from her personal email. The stress of all this had exhausted her and she took a long nap. Alex and his buddies had enjoyed such good luck the day before that they had gone fishing again today so she had the place all to herself. He returned about 8:00 PM without a catch. Their luck had not been as good this time out.

She arrived at the office a little later than usual the next morning and Roger was already there. He was regaling a group with tales of his own week of fishing on a lake in Oregon. He told them that an old college buddy had called him unexpectedly a few days before and asked him to spend the week with him up there. He told them that he and his imaginary friend had been great buds in college and he just couldn't turn down the offer. They had fished, cooked out over an open fire every night and recalled countless memories from their days at the university. It sounded very plausible and everyone was eating up the stories that he spun.

As she listened to all of this Valerie found herself being taken in and believing the story that Roger was telling. He wasn't usually that spontaneous of a guy but maybe he would make an unplanned trip to reunite with an old buddy. She knew he enjoyed fishing as much as Alex did and he loved to spend time at lakeside cabins and explore new areas when on vacation. She really wanted to believe him but at the same, she had her doubts. Her intuition was working overtime to convince her that this was just a big show and something else had drawn him away last week. In a way it didn't matter. He was back now. And she had one more step to take in her personal mission for Alex.

The group finally broke up and everyone started delving into their Monday morning routine. She and Roland met with Roger and brought him up to speed on what they had done during his absence. They reviewed several reports with him and clarified a number of questions that he had. They were dismissed around lunch time, but then she spent a good part of the afternoon working closely with Roger to prepare their presentation for an upcoming board meeting. He seemed perfectly normal, giving no signs of anything outside the ordinary.

By 4:00 PM they had finished their preparation and he told her he was leaving a little early today. Since he had been gone for a week he planned to take Darcy, Jillian and Evan out to dinner tonight to catch up with them. He was planning to take them to a place they all enjoyed where a variety of South American themed pizzas were served by gauchos and they even had dessert pizzas. It was one of the few places they could all agree on and have a good time. She told him that sounded great and wished him a goodnight.

By the end of the next hour the floor was almost deserted and she entered his office pretending to look for something. She soon found his personal laptop which he had not bothered to take home with him and logged onto it. She searched through the folders and files just as thoroughly as she had his corporate PC and found nothing that seemed of any use. She went through his email inbox, sent mail and trash and found nothing pointing to correspondence with an offshore bank and nothing relating to passports or fake id's. She even dug into his browser history and found nothing of interest, not even any links to porn sites. If he was using this laptop for such things, he was being extremely cautious and leaving no clues behind.

Just as she was about to log off and give up she noticed one folder she had overlooked. It was simply named FREE. Opening it she found one file, a Word Document that was labeled "passwords". She couldn't believe it. Alex had said many people did this to remember all their passwords but it just seemed too easy. She tried to open the file but it was password protected. What password would he use? She tried his login passwords and they didn't work. She looked at the folder name and tried "freedom". It opened and a list of passwords appeared before her. What they gave access to was unclear but that was okay. She copied it to a thumb drive which she would give to Alex. He could use his expertise to unlock whatever secrets they held.

She put everything carefully back as it had been and walked back to her cubicle. She was thrilled to have found something that might be useful to Alex but she was anxious to get out of the building. She felt like a thief in the night.

CHAPTER EIGHT

The elevator door opened and she started to enter the compartment when she suddenly stopped and retreated to the office. While waiting for the elevator she had remembered one place that she had failed to look. She was sure that nothing would be there but she also knew it would keep nagging at her if she failed to look. Roger had a small compartment on the end of his bookcase where he kept a few bottles of liquor and two or three glasses. She had known what was in there and assumed there was no reason to look but now she thought that she might as well open it up and peer in so that no possibility was left untried.

She opened the door and saw the liquor and glasses in front but was surprised to see a small lockbox behind them. She picked it up and rattled the container. It sounded like papers and stuff was in there. The lock was a combination lock and she had no idea what the combination might be. It would not match any passwords since they contained letters and special characters. Finally she tried his employee badge number but it failed. What else might he use? She could only think of one other possibility, his birthdate. Moving the dial to 102376 she pulled the lid and it opened! His Social Security Card and a few other business cards were in there including one with the name of an officer at a bank in the Cayman Islands. Then at the bottom she hit gold.

She opened the passport and saw his picture with the name William Tyson. It was stamped with two entries from last week, one to New Zealand and another to Vanuatu. So the trip to Oregon had actually been a week in a place called Vanuatu. She had heard of that country and assumed it was close to New

Zealand but she really knew nothing about it. Along with it lay a driver's license with the same name. The final discovery was found under these two documents, a debit card for that same bank in the Cayman Islands.

So good old Roger was just as dirty as Alex had suspected. She still didn't want to believe it but the evidence left no doubt. She had come to suspect over the years that his home life was not very happy but she would never have guessed he would go to this extent to escape from it. She took pictures of all of these documents with her phone and put everything back just as she had found them. This time she scooted out the door and into the elevator and never looked back.

Alex was already home when she reached the apartment. She shared everything she had found with him and he explained that Vanuatu was a country with no extradition treaty with the United States. In fact you could even buy a citizenship there with no questions asked and have the protection of the government. He was also familiar with the bank represented by the debit card. It was often used as a haven by drug dealers and others to stash their cash. He told her he would go over the lengthy list of invoices tomorrow but there seemed to be little doubt that Roger was in deep trouble.

Alex in fact spent the next few days going over the invoices in detail along with other information he was able to obtain from what Valerie had given him. He wanted to tie as much to Roger as possible before confronting the man and taking the next steps. Finally on Thursday evening he told her that he had all he needed to make an arrest. He also told her to get the passport, license and debit card and bring them home with her the next day.

She agreed and hoped they were nearing the end of this ordeal.

They had dinner in the apartment that evening and she thought they were going to settle in for the evening, but instead Alex sat down on the sofa next to her and said, "Val, we need to have a talk. I want to tell you in more detail how this is going down and make sure you're prepared for it".

She thought everything was pretty much settled but answered, "Okay, sure. I guess we're in for quite a ride the next few days."

"You have no idea."

She thought to herself "no I guess I don't. I've never been part of an FBI sting before."

Alex then explained his plan to her in detail. Yes there was indeed much more to this than she had even considered. The more she heard, the more fascinated she became by Alex's narrative.

*

The next day she returned to the office and worked closely with Roger to complete their presentation for the board meeting. She struggled to appear normal and not show her emotions and though it was difficult, she thought she pulled it off quite well. If Roger noticed any anxiety on her part he never mentioned it. As the hours passed and quitting time approached she found herself getting more and more nervous. She couldn't wait for Roger to leave so that she could obtain the items that Alex had asked her to get. Finally the hour came and Roger left. They were the last two to leave the floor that evening and she texted Alex as soon as Roger exited and then went into his office and retrieved the items. She then texted a "thumbs up" emoji to Alex indicating she had them in hand.

Roger meanwhile rode down the elevator to the parking garage and was about to get in his sedan when a man walked up to him and held up what appeared to be law enforcement credentials.

"Roger Carlson, I'm Alex Stroud with the FBI and you are under arrest for embezzlement."

He looked at the man facing him and had no idea that he was the boyfriend of his assistant Valerie. She had never shared anything about having a boyfriend, much less living with someone else.

Roger stood by the open car door and listened in frozen amazement as this man read him his rights. He quietly acknowledged that he understood his rights and waited to see what would happen next. His mind next went to what seemed like a strange place as he briefly pondered why it was the FBI and not state officials arresting him, but then he reflected that his company and its subsidiaries had several contracts with the federal government and that must make it a federal crime.

He was now starting to compose himself a little bit and he blurted out in desperation, "Look, I don't know what you're talking about. I'm the Chief Accountant of this company. I haven't done anything wrong. You've made a big mistake."

"Well Mr. Carlson, we'll sort that out and give you a chance to explain everything. But right now you're taking a ride with me and I have to handcuff you. Please turn around and face the car and put your hands behind your back."

Tears filled Roger's eyes as he obeyed the agent. This was not the way he had planned his freedom. He had been so careful. How in the world had they managed to catch on to him after all these years? It was the perfect plan. How could it have failed?

He took a seat in the agent's car and asked, "Where exactly are we going? I need to contact my attorney and I won't be making any statement without him."

"We're going to one of our field offices and you can call the attorney when we get there."

He looked out the window and tried to think of his next steps as the car made its way through downtown rush hour traffic.

CHAPTER NINE

Valerie waited at the gate as they called out the row numbers that were now allowed to board the plane. She had only brought a carry-on bag for the flight and carried it down the aisle where she found her seat. Stuffing the bag in the overhead compartment she sat down next to the window and stared out at the tarmac. She was exhausted from the last few days and felt like she deserved a vacation like never before. So much had happened. And it had all happened so quickly.

Boarding was almost completed when a nice looking gentleman sat down in the aisle seat beside her. Nobody had purchased the middle seat in their row. He nodded to her and smiled and said "So, it's a long flight to New Zealand. Have you flown it before?"

"No, it's my first time but I understand it's about twenty hours. I've never had a flight that long before. Have you?"

"Can't say that I have. Is this for business or pleasure?"

"Oh, it's a vacation. I'm very excited. I'm actually going to Port Vila in Vanuatu from Auckland."

"Really? That's a coincidence. So am I. I'm actually on vacation myself."

"Well, it's a long flight. We might as well get to know each other. My name is Bridgette Nelson."

"It's a pleasure to meet you, Bridgette" said Alex. "My name is William Tyson."

The plane door closed and the flight attendants started their safety overview as it taxied down the runway. Within a few minutes Alex and Valerie, or William and Bridgette, were airborne.

An hour into the long flight Valerie switched to the middle seat and whispered to Alex, "Looks like everything is working like you planned."

"So far so good, Bridgette. And remember we must never use our real names again. We are William and Bridgette."

He quietly explained to her that Roger was no longer in custody. He had agreed to trade his freedom for the money he had so carefully embezzled over the years. He would take the resignation letter that Valerie had composed and turn it in for her. With his contacts Alex had been able to switch the photograph on Roger's fake passport and driver's license and Roger had given him the Pin Number for the debit card. Using those same contacts he had also expedited fake documents for Valerie in the name of Bridgette Nelson. In return Alex promised him that he and Valerie would disappear and he could resume his life as if nothing had happened.

Valerie listened to all of this and marveled that her law enforcement boyfriend had been able to put all of this together in such a short time. That Thursday evening when Alex had sat with her on the sofa and explained his real plan to her she couldn't believe what she was hearing. At first she had objected and said, "No, no Alex. That's just making us thieves. We'll end up in prison instead of Roger." But the more she listened the more impressed she was with Alex's plan. He had thought of every little detail it seemed, right down to planning both of their resignations from their current jobs and obtaining fake ID's . He convinced her that the huge conglomerate where she worked would never miss the money because Roger had executed the embezzlement so well. Finally after two hours of back and forth she agreed to go along with her boyfriend's plan. Her only stipulation was that Roger would not be harmed or arrested if he cooperated with them. Alex assured her that would be the case.

She was glad that Roger had cooperated. She still liked Roger and wished him no harm. Perhaps he would now do what most guys do and just get a divorce and start a new and happier life for himself. That was certainly what she was doing. She rested her head on William's shoulder and closed her eyes.

Eight hours of looking out the window at the ocean and twelve hours of napping later, they arrived on time in Auckland New Zealand and after a two hour layover they boarded a plane for their final destination, Port Vila Vanuatu. They were both exhausted when they arrived and immediately went to the hotel and checked in. You would think twelve hours of sleep on the plane would have been plenty but it simply wasn't the same. They slept until the next morning and then arose and had breakfast served on the balcony of their room overlooking the Pacific Ocean.

The next several days were quite busy as they shopped for a permanent place to live. They could now afford to live anywhere they chose on the island and build their dream house. But they opted instead to be more discrete and leased a nice condo on the beach. It had large bedroom suite, a small second bedroom that they could use as an office, a lavish living room that looked out over the ocean and a well-equipped kitchen. It was everything they needed and then some.

In addition to finding a permanent residence they both needed complete wardrobes, although it would be much more casual than the ones they had left behind. Bridgette had never been a shopaholic but she had also never had an unlimited budget. She found herself enjoying the indulgence, picking out clothes for every day, for the beach, for more formal occasions. She wasn't sure when she would need the more formal attire but she could imagine that they must have a theatre with plays and musicals, symphonies and etc. Life on the beach was great but she planned to enjoy these other distractions as well.

Finally they went to a government office where William led the conversation. They talked to an official and obtained an application for citizenship. She was shocked later when William told her that the cost was $150,000 for each of them. But he assured her that it was well worth the $300,000 and besides to remember that they had over $80,000,000 and the fee was only a tiny percentage of that. She knew that he was right. He had also paid a small bribe to the official to speed up the process and they had their papers within two weeks of applying.

William bought a very large and nice boat for them to scoot around the islands on and to fish from. She had only vaguely heard of Vanuatu before all of this and was surprised that it consisted of nearly eighty islands and in addition to fishing the country offered scuba diving at many coral reefs, underwater caverns and even some old shipwrecks to explore. She was a good swimmer but had never gotten into scuba, but now she was excited to delve into this new hobby.

Today she sat on the beach outside of their condo, sipping on a Mai Tai, and reflecting on how her life had changed so much in such a short time. And even though Roger had failed to attain his own dream of freedom, no one had been hurt. He was free to move on with his life just as she and William were starting their new one.

CHAPTER TEN

Alex, now William, rose up from an afternoon nap and looked out the window of their condo. He saw Valerie, now Bridgette, lounging below on the beach and soaking up the sun. They had been in Vanuatu for almost three weeks now and he was starting to forget their old names and think of them both under their new monikers. Everything had gone exactly as he had planned and it appeared that they would live out their lives in this wonderful paradise. His only regret was that he had lied to Bridgette about the fate of the third party in their plan, Roger Carlson.

He had arrested Roger that evening in the parking garage and left in his agency car. They had not gone far when Roger must have realized that things did not look right. He asked cautiously, "Where are you taking me? Which FBI office?"

"Oh, sorry about that Roger. We have another stop to make first and I think you'll recognize it. When we get there, we're going to take another little ride and have a nice talk. You're going to make the decision of a lifetime."

"What the hell are you talking about? Are you really with the FBI?"

"Oh yes, I am."

They rode in silence after that until they got to the harbor and pulled to a stop in the parking lot near Roger's boat. It was about fifty yards from the parking lot, anchored in a slip on the water.

"Well that's my boat. Where are you taking me?"

"Like I said, we're going to take a nice ride and have the most important talk of your life. For now though I want you to shut up and walk to the boat with me. There's no one around right now and if you resist, I might have to plug you for trying to escape my custody."

Roger got very quiet and, if possible, even more concerned then and walked along in front of Alex towards his boat. They boarded the vessel and Alex unlocked the handcuffs and gave Roger the coordinates where he was to drive the boat. They went about two miles out to an area that Alex had predetermined after doing a little independent research.

They reached the spot and Alex had Roger anchor the boat. He then told him what he and Valerie had found, though he never revealed that Valerie was his source. He might as well let her have the peace of knowing that Roger never knew about her betrayal. He had even brought a knapsack containing the paper evidence that he had accumulated and showed it all to Roger.

When he had revealed the case he had against him, he looked Roger in the eye and said, "So, Roger there you have it. I only need one thing from you now. Give it to me and you go home today. Don't give it and you spend the next 30 years or so in Federal lockup. And if you get a lighter sentence than that, I'll make sure the state boys are aware and they can send you to a state prison for an additional stay."

"Oh God, I've worked so long, so hard to do this and now you're just taking it away. I haven't hurt anybody. Isn't there something we can do to work this out?"

"I'm afraid not. I agree you haven't really hurt anyone including that conglomerate you stole from. But the law is the law. Now, do you want to help yourself or not?"

"What is it that you need?"

"You know that Cayman bank may not be too cooperative with us trying to get that money back. So if you give me the passcode to your debit card, we can help you out and reduce this all to a healthy fine that you can pay and go home a free man. We'll even pay the fine out of the account so you're out nothing at all."

After much protesting and even trying to negotiate a few million to keep for himself, Roger finally saw that he had no alternative. Miserable as his life was at home, it beat prison. Given the situation he might even do what he should have done anyway and simply divorce his wife and pay whatever ridiculous alimony she was awarded. He gave the passcode to Alex who immediately tried it and ensured it was correct. Once he had accessed the account, he told Roger that the deal was done. Roger had one last question for him, "How did you guys ever get on to me? I was so careful all these years. No one should have known. How did I slip up?"

"Roger, I really wish I could tell you but I simply can't. But I will tell you that it was by a fluke. Your plan was quite good and well thought out."

Roger seemed to take a little pleasure in hearing this. He sat down on a seat by the steering wheel and hung his head for minute. When he looked up he was surprised to see a pistol pointed at him.

"What are you doing? I did everything you ask! What are you doing?"

"I know you did Roger but I was the one lying. I will soon be retiring from the FBI and enjoying the life you dreamed."

"Oh no! Don't do this! I won't tell anyone!"

The bullet hit squarely in Roger's heart. Alex quickly picked up the body and threw it overboard. He watched for a few minutes as the fresh blood almost immediately drew the attention of several sharks that started vying for their portion of the fresh meat. He had used an app on his phone that tracked shark sightings to get these coordinates and had then instructed Roger to steer the boat to the coordinates. He didn't know why they were congregated here and he didn't really care. He just knew that they would make sure that ole Roger was never found.

He now took Roger's cell phone and sent an email to the corporate HR Department informing them that Roger had received a resignation notice from Valerie who was resigning immediately due to some family emergency. He would send them the actual notice from her on Monday when he returned to the office.

He had actually given his own notice to the FBI when he hatched this idea and had even sold his interest in his boat to the other two agents.

Alex then went to the back of the boat and opened a storage area in the floor of the boat that contained a rubber life raft. There was a small air pump in the compartment and he quickly inflated the raft. Grabbing a couple of oars lying next to the raft he pushed it over the side and carefully got in and seated himself in the raft. It was a couple of miles to shore and he was glad he had been working extra time on the rowing machine in his gym. Going against the current he was nearing the shore about thirty minutes later when he stripped off his coat and jumped in the water. With a knife he always carried in his pocket, he punched a hole in the raft and turned and watched the water start to fill it. It would be underwater soon. He then swam the short distance left to shore and walked about a mile down the beach to his car. Opening the trunk he got out a fresh set of clothes he had stashed there and changed in the car. He tossed the old, wet clothes in a trash can and drove home to the apartment.

He trusted that Roger's wife would report him missing later that night or the next day or perhaps someone would just spot the abandoned boat and report it to the Coast Guard. Either way the subsequent investigation would likely determine that Roger had somehow fallen from the craft and disappeared. Hopefully he had left a ton of life insurance for his family.

Now as he walked down to the beach and took a seat next to Bridgette he thought to himself that *yes this is something she can never know. It would haunt her for the rest of her life.*

Bridgette looked at him and took his hand. They sat there looking out at the ocean, holding hands for several minutes. "This is so beautiful, so peaceful. I can't believe that we get to spend the rest of lives this way."

"It is wonderful, isn't it? You can thank your friend Roger for it. He's a very smart man and he really did have the perfect plan. For us."

Friday Night Lights

by
Bobby J Watson

"It is a painful thing to look at your own trouble and know that you yourself and no one else has made it."

— <u>Sophocles</u>

CHAPTER ONE

It was a chilly November Friday night in Texas and that could only mean one thing: Friday night lights. Football, especially High School football was almost a religion for many in the Lone Star State. And late November meant that winning teams were vying for a spot in the state playoffs. That was definitely the case for Jeremy Mason and his teammates on the Mustangs. The Mustangs represented one of the largest schools in Fort Worth and Jeremy as quarterback had led them to a near perfect season. With only one loss on their record, they just needed a win tonight against the Lions, a team from a nearby suburb, to go the playoffs where they planned to avenge that one loss and become the 1994 state champions.

However with only 12 seconds left on the clock they were down by four points, but Jeremy had led them down field from their own twenty-seven yard line to the opponent's eight where they faced a 2nd down and goal. Jeremy was confident as he crouched behind his center and prepared to receive the snap. The snap came and with ball in hand he faded back into the pocket. His line held the opposing Lions as he looked for an open receiver.

Austin Fellows, his favorite receiver, ran straight from his wide receiver position to the end zone and then cut to his left toward the corner. Jeremy threw a strike his way and could feel the exhilaration building as he watched the ball spin toward Austin. But just as it reached him a defender from the Lions jumped up out of nowhere and snagged the ball. Jeremy's heart sank as did the heart of everyone on the Mustangs and every one of their fans in the stands. That was it. Their season was over.

The player who made the interception didn't try to run the ball back. There was no need. The game was over. The Lions were headed to the playoffs. The Mustangs were headed home. No, he didn't try to run the ball back but instead he ran directly to Jeremy who just stood there in shock as the player ran right up to him and shook the ball in his face! He taunted Jeremy, yelling "Loser, Loser" at him repeatedly until his Lions teammates came and lifted him up on their shoulders as they ran to mid-field and started celebrating.

Jeremy watched as they ran away and the shock started to leave him. Losing the game was terrible. It was a hurt that would stay with him for a long time, perhaps forever. Yes, losing was bad but why did that guy have to rub it in like that? Watching their celebration and replaying the insulting jabs of that player in his mind, he became more and more angry. Losing was one thing, but being taunted like that was just wrong.

Finally he and the rest of the team retreated to their locker room. The coach was just as disappointed as they were, maybe more so. But he reminded them what a great season they had experienced. They could be proud; they had only lost two games all year and very few teams could say that. They should hold their heads up high and be proud of what they had accomplished. These accolades would normally have been nice to hear, but Jeremy barely even heard them. He kept thinking about that stupid idiot who had waved that ball in his face and called him a loser over and over.

He did snap out of it some when he heard the coach call his name. He was calling the names of all the seniors who had just played their last game, many of whom were heading to different universities on scholarships. Jeremy was one of those. He had received a full ride to one of the larger schools in Texas and would be the quarterback on their freshman team next season.

The coach then said something that really made him perk up and listen. It was directed specifically at him. The coach said,

"Jeremy, I know that last play really stung but take a little solace in knowing that young man who intercepted your pass was Brian Kitsworth, one of the top recruits in the nation and he'll be playing for Notre Dame next season." There was some murmuring from the other players as they seemed to recognize the name.

Jeremy nodded and said "Thanks Coach that helps", but he really didn't mean it. The coach then gave a few instructions for meeting the following Monday to turn in any equipment and wrap things up for the season and then he left. The players showered and got into their street clothes and left in groups of two or three. Finally only Jeremy was left. Some of the guys had asked him to go to one of their homes where they were going to shoot some pool but he had told them not tonight.

Alone now, he went into the coach's office and found a phone book and turned to the section for names ending in K. The Lions were from a nearby suburb that was included in the phone book. He found the address pretty quickly. Kitsworth was not a common name and there was only one address in that city the matched the name.

His anger had only grown as he listened to the coach and dressed in his street clothes. He was a good football player. He was headed to a major school just like this Kitsworth and he deserved an apology. He was going to go to the other school and wait. They would be later getting dressed and heading home since they had taken a bus to the Mustangs home field. He didn't want to make a big scene but he planned to follow Kitsworth and demand his apology. If he missed him at school, he knew where the guy lived. If he wouldn't apologize, then let come what may. He deserved an apology.

Traffic was light at that time of night and he arrived at the school parking lot after a twenty minute drive. He parked his Chevy pickup away from other cars but where he could see players coming out of their locker room and getting into cars and pickup trucks. He had gotten a good look at Kitsworth when the guy was right in his face. He would never forget the face of that creep. Several guys came out but none were Kitsworth. Had he come out before Jeremy arrived? Players continued to straggle out, mostly laughing and having a good time. Why not? They were headed to the playoffs. Finally it seemed that everyone had made their exit and Jeremy prepared to leave and drive to Kitworth's home to wait for him. But then who should come out but the punk himself? He was probably so conceited that even his own teammates hated him. Whatever, this was perfect.

Jeremy slowly drove his truck toward him as Kitsworth walked toward the only car left in the lot. Jeremy pulled alongside him as he walked and Kitsworth came to a halt and looked as Jeremy stopped and rolled the passenger window down. Kitsworth looked in, expecting to see a friend. Jeremy raised his voice and said, "Hey Jackass! Remember me?"

Kitsworth peered in and then grinned. "Oh yeah, the loser. Did you come here so you could get whipped again?"

"No, I came here so you could apologize. You won the game, but you didn't have to be a total jerk about it. Apologize and I'll forget it. Otherwise let's have it out right now."

"I owe you nothing. You wanna get whipped again? Come on out here and let's get it on."

With that Jeremy opened his door and started around the front of the truck. Kitsworth was already rounding the front of the truck and met Jeremy with a punch to the gut that doubled him over. Jeremy struggled for breath and straightened up to deliver his own blow, but just like in the game Kitsworth came out of nowhere with a right to Jeremy's temple and another gut punch that put him on the ground.

"Haha! This is great. I could do it all night long but I have a party to go to tonight. A winner's party!" With that he turned and started toward his car which was about thirty yards away.

Jeremy struggled to get up but finally managed to get back on his feet. Tears ran down his face, not so much from the pain but from the anger boiling inside. He couldn't let this punk just walk away! Somehow he managed to catch his breath enough to run toward Kitsworth who heard him coming and turned as Jeremy reached him. Kitsworth swung a haymaker. But this time Jeremy was ready. He went low as Kitsworth swung. Jeremy rammed his head into his enemy's stomach and brought him to the ground. He hit him on each jaw before his opponent knew what was happening. This only intensified Jeremy's anger and now he grabbed Kitsworth by the hair and slammed his head against the pavement. Over and over he slammed his head and yelled "Now who's the loser? Now who's the loser?" The last thing Kitsworth saw was the image of Jeremy, crazy with anger, yelling "Now who's the loser?"

Jeremy finally stopped and just stared down at the face on the pavement. Slowly the anger subsided and looking at the blood pooling under the face he thought *What have I done! My God, what have I done! I wanted an apology, not this!*

He tried to rouse the body but it was no good. He knew that he had killed the other player. Yes, the guy was a jerk but this was never what he intended. *What should I do now? Should I find a pay phone and call 911?*

Finally he decided to just go home. Kitsworth was dead. Someone would find the body. Would they trace it back to him? He drove away toward home and pulled into an all-night convenience store and gas station. He went inside to the restroom which was empty and washed his hands and face. There was blood all over his hands. He must have washed and dried them ten times before grabbing a handful of paper towels and returning to his truck. The cashier was watching TV and barely noticed him coming or going. He took the towels and rubbed down the steering wheel as assiduously as he had washed his hands. Finally he drove home. He went inside where his parents were already asleep. He lay in bed all that night replaying everything in his mind. What should he do? He really didn't know.

CHAPTER TWO

Isaac White had just finished his shift as night cook at a popular eatery and was driving home. He normally worked the day shift which started at 10:00 AM before the restaurant opened at 11:00 for lunch. But he had traded shifts with another cook who would take his place tomorrow. He often took a shortcut by the high school before hitting the main highway that took him home. As he drove down the lonely street his thoughts were on his two kids. Tomorrow was a rare Saturday off from work and he planned to take them to the Fort Worth Zoo. Fort Worth might be thought of as a cow town and it did play that theme up for tourists, but it also had one of the top ten zoos in the nation and his kids loved going there.

Rounding a curve in the road at the edge of the school parking lot he spotted something lying on the pavement. His headlights brought the object into direct view and he saw that it was a body! Isaac immediately stopped his car and rushed to the young man lying there. He had received some limited medical training while in the army and checked for a pulse but found none. *Who is this young man,* he asked himself. *What had happened here?* There was a large pool of blood under the boy's head and Isaac put a hand on each side of the head and raised it up to inspect the wound. Just as he did this a bright light shone from behind him and an officer yelled "Put your hands up and get away from the body!"

Andrew Worthington and his partner had been on routine patrol when they happened on the scene. Like Isaac they checked the body for a pulse and called for an ambulance even though they knew it was too late. They handcuffed Isaac and put him in the back seat of the patrol car. They told him to wait there while they called detectives to come to the scene. Isaac protested, "I just found that boy! I was just checking the wound. I was going to find a pay phone and call 911! Please officers, please believe me."

"Well that may be so. But then again maybe you saw a lone white boy and thought he might have some cash on him. But he fought back and you killed him."

"So that's it, huh? A black man finds a dead body so he must have killed the guy. Man, I got a job. I don't need to rob nobody. Please believe me officer."

"Yeah well, you can try running your story by the detectives when they get here. Shouldn't be long now."

Within the next five minutes the detectives arrived along with a crime scene van carrying two technicians. The ambulance also arrived and the medics confirmed that the victim was deceased. The technicians then cordoned off the area and took photos of the scene from several different angles. The Medical Examiner had come to the scene shortly after the crime scene team and he now examined the body. He found the preliminary cause of death to be due to the victim's head being smashed repeatedly against the pavement and estimated that death had occurred within the last two hours. There were no real surprises in his report. Of course an autopsy would be performed and would state the official cause of death.

The crime scene techs then drew an outline around the body for future reference and began collecting evidence. Crime scene investigators are guided by Locard's Exchange Principle which essentially states that every contact between people leaves a trace. In accordance with that principle they now collected blood samples, shoe prints, and tire tracks. They also looked for latent finger prints although the paved asphalt environment offered little hope of finding any of value. All of these items were carefully entered into an inventory log for the crime.

Meanwhile the detectives listened to Isaac's story and called the restaurant to confirm that he had worked that evening. However everyone had left work by the time they called and they said they would check back the next morning. They asked if he had seen anyone else in the parking lot and he said that there was no one else there but the body. They asked a few more questions before arresting him and informing him of his rights.

They then transported him to the jail where he was photographed and booked. He used his one phone call to tell his wife what had happened. She shrieked into the phone in disbelief. How could they think Isaac had done such a thing? What would she tell their sons? Finally he shared that the detectives said he would probably not be arraigned until Monday and he would try to let her know more as he learned it. His last words to her were simple, "I didn't do this thing. Please pray for me, for us that they realize that."

CHAPTER THREE

Jeremy tossed and turned in his bed all night. Normally a sound sleeper who would not wake up and dress until close to noon on the morning after a ballgame, he got up this Saturday at 8:30. He might have gotten two hours sleep in bits and pieces throughout the night. He had a television in his bedroom and turned it on with the volume set low so his parents wouldn't know he was awake. He might normally have turned to ESPN or even some silly cartoon but today he turned to a local channel where the news was on. He was anxious to hear if Brian Kitsworth had been found or not.

The station reported about some crisis in the Middle East and then something about a deadlock in Congress over a funding bill. He could care less about either of those right now. The Middle East always seemed to be in turmoil and he didn't really even understand what a funding bill was although it sounded like it had something to do with money. Finally they got to the local news and sure enough it was the first story told, but what he heard shocked and confused him.

The news anchor reported, "The body of a high school football player from Arlington was found on the school parking lot last night. The name of the young man has not been released pending notification of next of kin. Foul play appears to have been involved and police have arrested a man who was found at the scene. The name of the suspect has also not yet been released, but we did learn that he will be arraigned for Capital Murder on Monday."

What? Jeremy couldn't believe what he was hearing. *Everybody was gone but Kitsworth. Who could have still been there? Someone's been arrested for what I did! No! No! This can't be happening.* These thoughts raced through his mind and he actually started panting, short of breath as the anxiety weighed upon him. Then he thought that *surely they'll realize that this person didn't do it and let him go. My God, what have I done?*

Finally he went downstairs where his parents had finished breakfast and were having coffee while watching some old western on television. This was how they spent nearly every Saturday morning, but they were surprised to see Jeremy so early.

"What are you doing up so early, son?" his dad asked.

"Oh, I just couldn't sleep after that game last night. I thought we had it won until that very last play."

"We did too. That was a tough one for sure. That kid just came out of nowhere and his attitude was terrible. I hope his coach got on to him for the way he waved that ball in your face."

"I know. I guess he was just excited."

His mother then chimed in, "Would you like me to fix you some bacon and eggs for breakfast, dear?"

"No, I'll just have some Cheerios and orange juice."

"You sure? I can make you something."

"No, I'm good but thanks."

He fixed a bowl of cereal and a glass of juice and sat at the kitchen table slowly munching on the cereal. He thought to himself *what should I do? Should I tell my parents what I did? It would kill them. Their honor roll, scholarship quarterback a murderer. No, he couldn't tell them. Should he go to the police and tell them what happened? Yes, that's what he should do but he couldn't convince himself to do it. Let's just see how this plays out. Surely they'll let the guy go.*

Meanwhile Isaac sat in his jail cell. He and the other prisoners had been served breakfast early that morning. He still couldn't believe this was happening. He was just driving home from work and had stopped when he saw someone in trouble and now he was confined to this small cell with bars facing him. A deputy came and opened the door and told him that he had a visitor. He trudged alongside the deputy to a room where he could sit on one side and speak to his wife through a glass partition on the other side. He had never seen her look so scared and nervous.

He explained everything to her as best he could. She was still in disbelief and didn't know what to say or do. They talked about a lawyer but there was no way he could afford a high-dollar attorney on his pay. They would have to ask for a public defender. They wouldn't know until the arraignment on Monday if bail would be possible or how much it would be. She told him that she had sent the boys to her mother for the weekend. She hadn't told them anything yet and wasn't sure how to tell them. Isaac assured her that she would find the right words and they were bright boys. They would understand. The deputy told them their time was up and she held her hand up to the glass. Isaac held his up opposite hers. It was as close to a kiss as they could manage.

The detectives came just before noon and took him to an interview room to go over his story again. He had seen enough crime shows on TV to say that he wouldn't be talking any more without an attorney. He also told them he couldn't afford one and would need a public defender. They left and reported this to their superior officer who called the public defender's office.

That afternoon he was again called to the interview room where he met Thomas Jenkins, his public defender. Jenkins was a slight young man with dark brown hair who wore round glasses and looked to Isaac to be about fourteen years old. *Oh boy* he thought to himself. *I hope this isn't the young man's first case, but even if it's not he can't possibly have tried too many.*

He then told his story to his attorney who listened carefully, asked few questions but took plenty of notes. Jenkins then told the detectives they were ready if the detectives wanted to question Isaac now.

CHAPTER FOUR

They didn't just let the guy go as Jeremy had hoped they would do. In fact they arrested Isaac White for murder in the first degree or capital murder as they call it in Texas. Jeremy kept watching for any news about the case, but there was little mention of it after the initial report and the arrest of White. He kept thinking that they just had to let the man go eventually. They had to realize their mistake. Short of news he set about trying to learn what he could about the man.

He went one Saturday for lunch at the restaurant where White had been a cook. It was a nice restaurant with a menu of American favorites and a nice atmosphere. The waiter was pretty friendly and talkative. After placing his order Jeremy asked if this was the restaurant where the guy had been arrested for murder.

"Yes, unfortunately this is the place."

"So what kind of guy was he anyhow?"

"I worked here with him for about a year. He was a terrific guy. Always friendly with everyone, never got upset. I was shocked when I heard what he had done.

"So you think he did it?"

"You know, they say the evidence is all there but it's just hard for me to believe. I never saw him get angry or physical or anything. Like I said a real shock. Well I need to get your order turned in, place is starting to get busy."

After lunch that same day he drove to the address he had found for Isaac White. It was a medium sized frame house in a nice, quiet middle class neighborhood. While he sat there a car pulled in the driveway and a woman and two young boys got out. The woman popped the trunk on the car and the boys each grabbed a bag of groceries. The woman led them inside and then the boys came back out and got another bag apiece. Isaac had been denied bail so it was just the three of them now.

Gosh they look like nice kids and a nice family Jeremy thought to himself. The guilt weighed heavily on him the rest of that day and night as he recalled the conversation with the waiter and saw the kids so politely carrying in groceries for their mom. *Surely he won't go to prison* he kept telling himself.

As time dragged on he began to wonder why it took so long for a trial to take place. The murder had occurred in November and now school was nearly out and still no trial. Then in late April they started the process of selecting jurors and the case hit the local news once more. The jury was seated pretty quickly and the trial began in early May.

Jeremy and his friends were nearing the end of their high school years and graduation was only a short time away when the state called their first witnesses. These witnesses were primarily coaches and students from Brian's football team who testified that they had celebrated their victory over Jeremy's school, and that most of the players had then gone to the home of one of the wide receivers to party and celebrate. Brian Kitsworth had received a phone call from the head coach at Notre Dame congratulating him on the victory and his game-saving play while the others were dressing and preparing to go to the party. Two of the players testified that they were the last two to leave and Brian had said he would be joining them shortly. They were surprised when he didn't show up at the party.

The detectives and a crime scene investigator then testified. Their testimonies were short and to the point. White had been found hovering over the body at the scene and had the young victim's blood on his hands and shirt when they discovered him. No other significant fingerprints, shoe prints or tire tracks had been found to indicate anyone else had been there. Since the crime occurred in an asphalt parking lot this was no real surprise.

Defense attorney Jenkins tried to show that these testimonies were not conclusive and someone else could have committed the crime before Isaac arrived on the scene but his efforts were pretty ineffective.

The defense called White's co-workers and others who served mostly as character witnesses and finally White himself took the stand in a last ditch effort to save himself. He gave an account of his actions that night and vigorously denied any involvement other than trying to help someone in need. The prosecutor hammered away at him on cross examination but Isaac stuck to his story and refused to admit to anything other than being a Good Samaritan.

Finally the case was turned over to the jury. Given the time they were out the jury must have elected a foreperson and enjoyed the lunch provided by the county before returning a unanimous verdict. Isaac White was guilty of Capital Murder. His wife shrieked at the announcement and was walked out of the room by a relative. Other family members and friends shook their heads in disbelief.

Shortly afterward the jury recommended a sentence of life in prison without the possibility of parole. They said they did this because Isaac had no previous criminal record and that led them to take the death penalty off the table.

Ironically the same day that a jury condemned Isaac White to spend the remainder of his life in prison, Jeremy was reaching a milestone of his own as he graduated from high school. After the ceremony and congratulatory hugs from his parents he attended a party held at the house of one of his friends. The friend was from a well to do family who provided a live band for the evening. So there was music and dancing around the outdoor swimming pool. Jeremy and his friends sneaked in some beer which they enjoyed, supposedly without the knowledge of his friend's parents. Some of the guys got wasted but Jeremy limited himself to two or three beers.

When he left the party that night he tuned his car radio to a local news station. Ordinarily he would have tuned to music, but lately when alone in the car he listened to the news in an effort to stay updated about the trial. After listening for a few minutes he heard the verdict. He couldn't believe what he heard. He had always wanted to believe that the police made very few if any mistakes, especially in a crime this bad. Obviously he now knew that the police were human as was the judge and jury. They could all make mistakes and they had just made a terrible one that cost Isaac White his life as a free man.

Again he asked *what am I to do? I can't let this happen but I don't want to go to jail either. I just wanted an apology. What am I to do?*

Of course he knew the answer to his question. Then he thought *I just graduated and I'm going to college. My life is just starting.* On what was supposed to be a happy night to remember, the guilt crushed down on him. He drove home and went to bed, burying his head in his pillow and trying to push the demons away.

CHAPTER FIVE

Jeremy spent the summer working as a life guard at a pool owned by a Homeowners Association. He had held this job the previous two summers and the pay was pretty good, plus it kept him busy which was what he needed most of all. Every day he thought about the fact that a man was behind bars because of him. Though working and staying busy helped the time go by, he couldn't escape the guilt completely. Some days he would try to rationalize what had happened. He would think *okay, so Isaac didn't commit murder but maybe he was guilty of some other crimes and deserved to be in prison. Maybe the police knew that and that helped convince them that he had murdered Kitsworth.* Of course he had learned enough about Isaac to know that this was probably nonsense and then reality would come back with its load of guilt.

In mid-August he reported to his new school. His parents accompanied him and helped him move into his room at the athletic dormitory. His mother could not have been prouder to see her son attending a major university. His father was beaming at the idea that not only was his son in college but he would be quarterbacking a major university team. Jeremy tried to share their joy and he acted the part, but he had lost the enthusiasm he once had for football. He would try his best but he just didn't have the spark that had driven him to success in high school.

His parents left after spending the night in a hotel and visiting him in his new room the next morning. The university was a community unto itself with nearly 50,000 students attending the school. He got to know some of his new teammates. Most of them seemed like swell guys and he knew he could fit in with them. It would have been nice if one of his high school buddies had also made the team, but most of them had gone to smaller schools. His roommate was a beast name Jamie Griffin. Jamie stood 6' 6" tall and weighed nearly 300 pounds. Needless to say he was an offensive tackle and despite his appearance he was actually a pretty nice guy and even seemed smarter than most would have expected. Jeremy liked him right away.

A few days after arrival the coaches gathered the freshmen together where they introduced themselves and all the players. They started practicing different drills and Jeremy was amazed at the talent this team possessed. There were good players in high school but the concentration of talent on a major university team was another level altogether. Occasionally he thought of Brian Kitsworth, who would have been practicing with the Fighting Irish at Notre Dame right now. Then his coach would yell an instruction and his thoughts would return to his own practice field.

The team's first opponent was against a smaller university that was known more for its academia than its football. It was an away game and Jeremy started the game at quarterback and threw two touchdown passes in the first quarter. The head coach soon started sending in second and third string players to give them their first taste of college ball. Even though his numbers looked good on paper Jeremy knew that his heart wasn't really in the game. This became more apparent the next week in practice when the coach on several occasions had to call his name three or more times before he even realized it.

The next game was against a much more competitive opponent but one that they still should beat pretty handily. Jeremy threw a touchdown pass on the first drive of the game but then threw two interceptions. On both occasions he called one play but then threw the ball for a totally different route. The coach pulled him and put in the second string quarterback. Fortunately the team managed to win despite his performance and the second stringer led the team to a 28-13 victory.

After the game the coach came up to him and said, "Son, I don't know if you had the jitters because it was your first game in front of the home crowd and your parents or what, but your head wasn't in that game. I expect better than that."

"Sorry Coach, I guess I was a little nervous. It won't happen again."

When they were back in their room Jamie said, "Tough one today dude. You'll get 'em next time. Hey, I know a frat house that's throwing a big party. Wanna come with me and grab a few beers?"

Normally Jeremy would have made some excuse not to go but tonight he didn't want to be alone and what better company than his huge protector. "Sure, sounds like fun. Let's do it." The party had plenty of beer, music and girls. Jamie danced with two or three different girls while Jeremy watched. He sipped on his beer and even chuckled a few times at the big behemoth dancing but he didn't feel like it himself. A few girls even approached him and he politely told them that maybe later he would dance with them.

Finally Jamie came back and sat down next to him. "What's up dude? You just sitting here? Can't get the game off your mind or what?" He looked at Jamie and spoke over the loud music. "Jamie, you ever do something you knew was wrong but you did it anyway and then you just can't quit thinking about it?"

The tackle just looked at him with a bewildered frown. "What, you mean like staying out after curfew or something? Sure, I did that a few times. No big deal."

Jeremy just smiled at him and shook his head. "You stay here and enjoy. I'm heading back to the room." He walked to the door leading outside and looked back. Jamie was dancing with yet another beauty. *Good for him* he thought.

Unfortunately his performances didn't improve and his mental lapses at practice persisted. Finally after the fourth game the coach called him into his office and demoted him to second string. He told him, "Son, I don't know what's going on with you. I've seen you play in high school. I know your talent level. You're the best quarterback on this team. Put your mind to it and you might even challenge the varsity QB. But there's something going on with you and until you figure it out you'll never reach your potential."

No matter how hard he tried, no matter what mind games he tried to play the images of Kitsworth lying dead on the parking lot pavement and Isaac sitting in a prison cell would not go away. At practice, during class lectures, no matter where he was, those two were there along with him. Finally the fall semester ended and he went home for Christmas break. His grades that semester were passing but not what they should have been. He was a much better student than they showed.

Finally he worked up his nerve and had a talk with his parents and told them that he was simply not happy there at the university. He said he had tried to fit in and make friends but he just didn't feel at home there. He told them that he wanted to transfer to a smaller school that was close by and that several of his old high school friends attended. Then he took a deep breath and looked at his dad and added that he was through with football. He just didn't have the passion for it anymore.

His mother was disappointed but said that his happiness was most important and if that meant changing schools then that was something she could accept. His father was beyond devastated. He had dreamed of his son being a star quarterback at a major university and maybe even playing in the NFL. And now he was throwing it all away and couldn't even really explain why? He finally threw up his hands and left the room saying, "I'll never get you Jeremy but okay. If that's what you want, okay. Go and do what you have to do."

CHAPTER SIX

Jeremy knew that his parents had limited resources and had expected his scholarship to pay for his college education. So he took off the spring semester and worked at a local grocery store stocking shelves and sacking groceries. Invariably some of the customers every day would recognize him and he would have to explain that he had dropped out of the university and planned to go to the other school next fall. And no, he wouldn't be playing football. One or two each day would then ask if he was injured or something and he would tell them that no, he just didn't like the bigger school and had lost his passion for football. That got some strange looks, especially from the men.

But he saved almost every dollar he made and accumulated enough to pay his tuition. He would have to take out a student loan to help with room and board and other costs, but he was determined to do it all himself. Finally the time came and he registered at the new school. He had decided to major in Mathematics but of course most of his classes were still the required general education courses. His new roommate was Stephen York. Steve was a good friend from high school and had been in the band instead of the football team. Jeremy was sort of glad to have a roomie who wasn't playing football.

He settled into his class schedule the first couple of weeks. He liked most of the professors and enjoyed the subjects. After that first couple of weeks he started looking for a part-time job to cover incidental expenses and save for the next semester. The on-campus jobs were taken but he found a position at a bookstore off campus. They carried many of the required course books at lower costs than the campus store plus it attracted several customers from the small town itself. He worked as a cashier and also kept the shelves stocked. Not the most exciting job but it met his needs.

One of his co-workers was a pretty freshman like himself named Julie Brewer. Julie was not only pretty with shiny black hair and sparkling blue eyes, but she was also fun to work with. Jeremy was drawn to her immediately and after working there a couple of weeks he worked up his nerve to ask her out on a date. They had dinner that first night at a hamburger place that was close to campus and popular with the students. Then they went to a place called Rink 'n Roll. It was a roller skating rink during the week and on weekend days, but on Friday and Saturday nights it converted into a venue for live bands and dancing. As they started dancing, Jeremy couldn't help it and started laughing uncontrollably. Julie looked at him wondering what in the world was going on and later he explained to her that when he started dancing he suddenly recalled the images of Jamie dancing with the girls at the frat house. Of course she didn't know Jamie but Jeremy's description of the big ox made her laugh too.

After that first night came more dinners at different restaurants, movies, dancing and finally they even went to a football game together. It was Jeremy's first game to watch since leaving the university. These dates were always fun but what Jeremy really liked was Julie's sensitivity and her real interest in him. Soon they were a steady item and he felt himself falling in love with her. They continued working at the bookstore together until the semester ended. Both returned to their homes for the summer where Jeremy again procured work at the grocery store. But before leaving the campus they pledged their love for each other and secured their jobs at the bookstore when returning in the fall.

Every night that summer Jeremy would call her and they would talk endlessly on the phone.

These calls were wonderful.   They actually talked about everything in their lives. Julie told him all about her childhood and growing up, what her parents were like and her high school days. He shared everything as well and especially about going to the university that one semester and how he had lost his love for football. She had no idea he had been such a star athlete but she seemed to understand his change of heart and his move to the smaller school. The only thing that he never told her about was Brian Kitsworth and Isaac White. He wanted to tell her and he determined to do so many times, but then he would get scared that she wouldn't understand and he would give in to his fears. He told himself that *this is the one burden I have to carry and live with just by myself.*

The next three years went by in a flash with them continuing their courtship attending classes and working at the bookstore. They also continued their long distance relationship every summer as they returned to their homes. The night before they were to graduate Jeremy took her to the nicest restaurant in the college town. They had steak and baked potatoes and shared memories of the last three and half years. It had been a sweet time for Julie and a healing time for Jeremy. He never forgot about Brian and Isaac; in fact he remembered them every day.   But now that memory was tempered by his love for Julie. Somehow being with her enabled him to set those haunting images aside and feel normal. When their dessert arrived Jeremy nodded to the waiter who uncovered the dish that supposedly contained a piece of chocolate cake, but to Julie's surprise the plate held only a single ring. When she looked up Jeremy was already on his knees and he asked her the magic question. She quickly said yes and pulled him up and into her arms. They kissed as the customers surrounding them applauded.

They were married the month following their graduation and rented a small house in Jeremy's hometown where he was hired as a math teacher at one of the middle schools. Julie became a teacher in the same district at what had been one of Jeremy's rival high schools. They quickly settled into life together as they began their careers.

Julie soon began visiting nearby churches and became a member of one only a few blocks away. All through their college days she had attended church every Sunday with rare exceptions. This was the one thing they did not seem able to share. Jeremy couldn't believe that a murderer who let someone else take his punishment belonged in church. Part of him wanted to go just to be with her but he could never take that step. But about a year into their marriage Julie became pregnant with their first child and she asked Jeremy to attend with her. She had never done this before but now she explained that she believed they should raise their children as church-going parents. Jeremy understood her reasoning and didn't really have a good excuse not to go so he started attending with her.

This church was different than the one his parents had occasionally attended when he was growing up. No one dressed up. Everyone was casual and the music was provided by a band that consisted of a lead and rhythm guitar, a bass guitar, a keyboard and drums. The music was upbeat and had a modern sound but a Christian message. The singers were the guy playing rhythm guitar and a young lady about their age.

The messages from the pastor, who wore jeans and a button down shirt hanging below his waist, were simple but provided good instruction for leading a Christian life. Jeremy found himself enjoying these services and the messages always gave him food for thought. After the first few visits he started looking forward to the next Sunday and wondering what the sermon would be about. After attending for a few months he made the decision to accept Christ as his Savior and, after conferring and confirming his beliefs with the pastor, he was baptized.

He now felt a freedom and a burden lifted like he had never known. He started attending bible studies one night a week with other men where they not only learned the bible, but shared their concerns and supported each other with prayer. One night he lay in bed alongside a sleeping Julie and thought about the changes in his life over the past several months. His faith in God was real and not just something he did for appearances. He truly believed that Jesus had died on the cross for his sins and that God had forgiven him. He knew that God had even forgiven him for what he had done to Brian and what he had failed to do for Isaac. God had forgiven him for this. Julie still didn't know but in his heart he knew she would forgive him. The only person who could never totally forget and forgive was Jeremy Mason.

CHAPTER SEVEN

It was mid-February when Julie gave birth to a 7 lb. 5 oz. baby boy. They named him Jonathan after Julie's favorite uncle. Julie was beaming as she held him in the hospital for the first time. Jeremy had never had younger siblings or been around babies very much. He held Jonathan with such care and protection you would have thought he was hugging a bottle of nitro glycerin. But his love for his new son was evident. There was a joy and happiness on his face that he had never before experienced. As they drove home from the hospital with the new family member, he thought about how much their life would change from this day forward and he was thrilled instead of terrified at what that meant.

When they arrived home he held Jonathan in his arms and took him to every room in the house as if he were giving a guided tour to a prospective buyer. He ended the tour at Jonathan's bedroom which had been fully equipped. Of course he would spend the first several nights in their bedroom before making the transition to his own. After showing Jonathan his room, Jeremy noticed a particular odor and rushed his son to Julie for a diaper change. He told her, "You know I do want to learn how to change diapers but for now I think you better take care of that". Julie laughed, "Okay sure buster. That works this time but starting with the next one you're going to start your training."

Over the next few years the bond between the three of them grew and grew. They were a happy family and Jeremy and his son were especially close. They watched children's shows on television together. They played with Jonathan's toys together. Whenever

Jeremy left the house to run an errand, Jonathan would cry and beg to go with him and he always got his way. When he got old enough they tossed a baseball back and forth as Jeremy taught him how to throw and catch. They went fishing together. Jonathan was too frightened to put live bait on the hook at first but he quickly overcame that and became a pretty good little fisherman.

They were inseparable and Julie tagged along with them whenever she could. At church they became known as the Triple J's: Jeremy, Julie and Jonathan. Sometimes he and Julie would confess that they should have had another child, but the three of them were so happy it seemed to make up for this. They were indeed a happy family.

When Jonathan was old enough, he started playing T-Ball and then he graduated to Little League. He had a good arm and better control than other kids his age. He also liked football but he didn't play. His passion was for baseball and that was okay with Jeremy. He would support him no matter the sport. After Little League ended at age twelve, Jonathan started playing Select League and they spent many weekends going to practices and tournaments throughout the state and sometimes even to neighboring states. Jonathan was developing into a star pitcher and those who remembered Jeremy's high school days commented that he had inherited his daddy's arm. When he finally reached high school he played on the school team and was the ace of that staff.

It's funny how things change over a period of time. Jonathan and his parents had always been so close and he had loved going to church with them. He loved the Bible stories and doing different crafts in Sunday School. As he grew older he really enjoyed going to camp with his church friends every summer. When he was eleven years old he was baptized. This came only after he discussed his decision with his parents and his pastor to ensure that he knew what this meant and that he was accepting Christ as his savior and following him. But during his late junior high years and especially after starting high school, things began to change.

He was no longer the happy kid that everyone had always known. He was often moody and he made excuses to not go to church. By the time he was in high school and had his own car, he quit going altogether. He would stay out past his curfew and began running with a crowd that Jeremy and Julie wished he would avoid. They chalked this up to normal teenage rebellion. They still loved their son as much as ever and thought this was a stage that would pass someday.

His attitude toward his dad changed more than anything else. They had once been so close, but now Jeremy could hardly hold a conversation with him. He seemed to resent anything that Jeremy said or tried to do. This was especially evident whenever Jeremy raised the subject of church. For whatever reason, his son had turned completely against the church and he actually told his dad that it was full of hypocrites and that Jeremy was the Chief Hypocrite in his opinion. When Jeremy asked him why he felt that way, Jonathan never gave a real answer but instead just shrugged and walked away.

While Jeremy and Julie felt that this teenage period would pass and someday their old son would return, they were concerned about his safety and that he would stay out of trouble. They prayed for this daily.

Secretly Jeremy agreed with Jonathan on one thing. He was a hypocrite. He still thought about Brian and especially Isaac every day. Julie had brought such happiness into his life that he didn't think about them as often as he used to do, but never a day passed that they didn't cross his mind. He could not have imagined how much this was about to change.

CHAPTER EIGHT

Jeremy had always been a reader and he had subscribed to the local newspaper for many years. He read the world, national and local news almost daily and he also kept up with whatever sport was in season. The crossword puzzle was one of his favorite things about the paper. He would often sit at night and work on it while Julie watched television. Sometimes she became a little irritated with him when he would watch just enough of a show to be interested and then ask her what had happened when he missed something because he was giving his attention to the crossword. He would just grin and tell her that he was multi-tasking and she would smile and fill him in on the scene he had missed.

With the digital age he had recently made the transition to the online version of the newspaper. One night he was reading on his tablet when a story caught his eye. The headline read "Murder Convict Has Terminal Cancer". He started to read the article and quickly saw that it was Isaac White who had cancer. It had spread from his kidney to his lungs and lymph nodes. The prison doctors were treating him, but they indicated that he had a year or so to live at the most. The article went on to say that he had maintained his innocence over the years, and it concluded by stating how devastated his family was about his prognosis.

All the guilt that he had ever felt seemed to coalesce into one huge boulder that crushed him. He turned pale and started shaking he head. Tears formed in his eyes. Julie was watching a reality show that she loved about people stranded on an island but she saw him reacting and asked him what was wrong. She thought he might be having a heart attack or something.

He shook his head and said, "No, I'm okay. Just had a sudden case of nerves thinking about one of the teachers at my school. He just learned that he has cancer. I'll be okay. I think I'll take a walk around the block to clear my head."

"Okay. You're sure you alright? I've never seen you get so upset."

"I'm sure. It's just that this guy is about my age and we talk almost every day. I guess we're pretty close" he lied.

He took that walk but the guilt only intensified. He asked himself how he had let this go for so long. He thought about Isaac's family and what they must be going through. *What if this was me? How would Julie and Jonathan be feeling now? It would kill Julie knowing this was happening and that I was innocent.* He couldn't vanquish these thoughts but he knew he had to control himself so Julie wouldn't worry about him. After two trips around the block he took a deep breath and went back inside. Julie immediately came up to him and wrapped her arms around him. He thought how much Isaac's wife must want to do the same right now.

He couldn't focus enough to teach the next day at school and he told his students in each class that today was a free day and they should work on their other homework or find something to read. He opened his tablet and kept it on the news story all day, reading it over and over. Isaac's wife Roberta reiterated his claim of innocence and maintained it was a terrible miscarriage of justice that he would die in a prison hospital. As Jeremy read this for the umpteenth time during his last period he made a decision. This had to end. It was wrong and it had to be corrected.

He did something after school that day which he had never done in nearly twenty years of marriage. He stopped at a local bar and had a drink. He had a shot of bourbon followed by a mug of draft beer. He knew what had to be done and this time he was going to go through with it. He realized that it would destroy Julie but he also knew it was the right thing and he couldn't put it off any longer. He finished his beer, popped a breath mint in his mouth, and started the drive home.

When he got there he was relieved to see that both Julie and Jonathan were home. He wanted to tell both at the same time and not have to repeat the story, except of course to the police. While still in his car he bowed his head and said a silent prayer that his family would understand and forgive him for what he had done and what he was about to do. Julie was undoubtedly worried about him because of the incident the night before and she greeted him with a kiss and a smile at the door. Jonathan was in his room with his ear buds on listening to music. Jeremy told Julie he needed to talk to both of them and she went and got Jonathan. The three of them then gathered in the kitchen.

Julie looked worried and thought that maybe his friend had taken a turn for the worse or even passed away. Jonathan just looked bored and irritated that they had interrupted his music for whatever this was. Jeremy wasn't sure where to start and finally just decided to go back all those years and start at the beginning.

"I have something to tell you both that isn't easy. In fact it's going to change all of our lives forever."

Julie now looked a combination of scared and bewildered. Jonathan just rolled his eyes and wondered why his dad was being so dramatic.

"Back when I was a little older than you Jonathan I did something terribly wrong. I was a senior in high school and as you both know I was the quarterback on my high school team. We almost made the state playoffs but we failed because on the last play of the game a guy on the other team named Brian Kitsworth intercepted my pass in the end zone. That was bad enough but he then came and practically rubbed the ball in my face and called me a loser. Losing was bad enough but he made it hurt even more and I couldn't get it off my mind so I went to his school and found him later that night as he left the locker room. I just wanted an apology but he taunted me instead and we got into a fight. I ended up slamming his head against the parking lot pavement and I killed him."

Julie's eyes were wider than he had ever seen them and she was so pale he thought she might faint. Jonathan said nothing.

"That's not the worst of it. I left the body on the parking lot and a man named Isaac White drove by and saw him. He got out of his car to render aid and the police showed up while he was leaning over the body. They arrested him and he's been in prison all these years. Now he's dying of cancer. He's a good man and I did this to him. Now I can't do this any longer. I'm going to the police tomorrow to confess."

Julie collapsed onto the sofa and held her face in her hands. Tears poured down her cheeks and on to the floor. She couldn't believe what she was hearing. He sat down by her and put his arm around her to comfort her. Even Jonathan stood behind the sofa and put his hand on her shoulder. Finally she looked up at Jeremy. "I just can't believe this. You're such a good man, Jeremy. I just can't believe it. You must have wrestled with this your whole life and I know you have to do this. I don't know what will happen but I will be there for you. I love you so much."

Jonathan now took his hand off her shoulder and stood straight up. He looked at his dad with contempt and said, "She can forgive you and I guess that's what a wife is supposed to do. But to me it just proves what I already knew. You're nothing but a liar and a hypocrite. Talking so much about God and all that and all the time you're just a murderer. I hate you and always will."

He then started toward the door. Jeremy followed him and tried to stop him but Jonathan slammed the door in his face and was soon in his car and out of the driveway.

"Just let him go" Julie said. "He's hurt right now but he'll come back."

Jonathan later texted his mother that he was at a friend's house and was spending the night.

The two of them just sat on the sofa the rest of the night. He hugged her and then she hugged him. Back and forth all night until dawn. Jeremy got up and showered and changed clothes while she made coffee. Then she went with him to the car and they drove to police headquarters.

CHAPTER NINE

Aimee Jinks walked into the detective squad room and headed straight for the coffee. She was glad to see that someone had arrived before her and brewed a fresh pot. She poured a mug of black coffee with no sugar and took a seat at her desk. She and her partner Edison Lomax were working a couple of cases, a bar shooting and a neighbor on neighbor murder but both were pretty straight forward. She was reviewing the Murder Books they had compiled on each case and adding clarifying notes where needed. Much of this would be the basis for prosecution of the offenders, both of whom had already been arrested. Her phone rang just as she took another sip from her mug.

She saw that it was from Jarrod Anderson, the Chief of Detectives for the Fort Worth Texas Police Department.

"Good morning, sir. What can I do for you?"

"Aimee, I have a gentlemen just came into my office and he is confessing to a murder."

The department had several cold cases but not that many currently active homicides so she asked, "What murder is that sir?"

"One that occurred around twenty years ago. Oh, and there's a man who has been in prison for that murder for almost the same length of time. This man says the inmate is innocent. I want you to hear his story and look into it. Make it your top priority."

Jinks answered in astonished amazement, "Yes sir. I'll come and get him right now."

128

She met Jeremy and Julie and escorted them to an interview room. Her first impression was that Jeremy was a man in his mid-forties and so he would have been pretty young when this murder occurred. Her second thought was that he didn't look like a murderer, but then who does?

She offered them both coffee and they both declined. She excused herself and went for a second cup. Returning to the room she asked if Julie was his attorney and he replied that she was his wife. He then stated that he did not have an attorney and would waive the right to one.

"Okay, well I need you to sign this waiver to that effect and then let's hear your story."

Jeremy recounted the events of that night again in as much detail as he could recall. Jinks made copious notes and asked a number of questions during the process. Jeremy had mentally prepared as much as he could for this and patiently answered each question to the best of his knowledge and ability. When he was finished, Jinks asked them to remain in the room and told them it might be several minutes before she returned. She could have arrested him and handcuffed him to the table or asked for an officer to watch the room but she had his address and she figured if someone came in to confess after all this time, they probably weren't going to make a run for it now.

Jinks returned to her desk and pulled up the old case on her computer monitor. She wanted to review it without them watching her and compare the details to the notes that she had taken. The similarities were striking. If Jeremy hadn't done this, he certainly knew a lot of the details, right down to what Kitsworth was wearing when he came out of the locker room that night. She even read an archived news story about the football game and it matched Jeremy's account. She had never had anyone come in and confess to a crime this old and wasn't sure what to do. Based on the information she had, she believed there was a very good possibility that Jeremy was telling the truth. She went and reported her findings to Chief Anderson and they decided to call in someone from the District Attorney's Office.

Todd McKellar was a seasoned veteran from the DA's Office and he arrived about an hour after he got the call. He had also looked up the case and reviewed it before coming over and now he took a seat opposite Jeremy Mason in the interview room. Just as with Jinks, he began by saying, "So Mr. Mason please tell me your story." Jeremy took a deep breath and again narrated the events of that night.

Meanwhile Jinks went to the Evidence Room and pulled what little there was on the case. DNA evidence did not come into play in Texas until a year or so after this crime and there were no viable samples for DNA testing. She reviewed the blood samples, shoe prints, and tire tracks that had been collected by the crime scene team that night. None of this evidence was conclusive and the conviction had been based mostly on the reports of the officers and detectives who testified that Isaac had been found kneeling over the body upon their arrival and shortly after the time of death. He had blood on his hands and clothes as if he had contact with the victim. All of this evidence was circumstantial and none of it disproved Jeremy's story.

She returned to the interview room where Jeremy was concluding his recall of the night for McKellar. She and McKellar excused themselves and went to Jinks' desk where they compared the stories they had heard and Jinks reported what she had found in evidence.

Jeremy had asked for a cup of coffee after giving his confession for the second time. He and Julie now sat in the room alone waiting to see what would happen next.

"God, I never dreamed how grueling this would be".

"I can't believe how well you've held up this morning. It must be terribly difficult, darling."

"It is. But in a way it's relieving also. After all of these years to finally unburden myself of this and let it be known."

McKellar and Jinks then reentered the room. McKellar said, "Mr. Mason I'm going to have to ask you to remain here while I report this to the DA and see what she wants to do next. It will be sometime in the afternoon before I come back with a decision."

Jinks then chimed in, "In the meantime it's getting close to lunch. I can get you something from the commissary. Here's a list of what they are offering today. Also, you've been in here all morning so if you need to visit the restroom, this is the time."

Jeremy and Julie took her up on both offers. They made their choices from the commissary and it was delivered to them. They sat in the room and ate and waited to learn their future.

McKellar drove to his office and met with the District Attorney. He reported everything to Jennifer Stinson the District Attorney for Tarrant County. After hearing his report, she asked him a simple question, "Do you believe him?"

"Yes, I do. He has no connection to Isaac White so there's no reason he would do this for him. And I could just see the relief pouring out of him when he confessed. He's kept this secret for all these years and it was liberating for him to tell it. Also as Detective Jinks pointed out to me, there is no hard evidence against either man. White was convicted on circumstantial evidence. And for what it's worth, White has always maintained his innocence."

"You know, with DNA and modern technology we've freed about fifteen men in the last two years who were wrongfully convicted of one crime or another. I wish there was something more tangible, but if you believe this guy, and the evidence doesn't contradict his story then I say let's arrest him."

"I agree."

"Now I have to get the wheels rolling to get that man out of prison and back home."

That process did not come easily but two months later Isaac White was given a full pardon and released from prison. He returned home to spend his final months with Roberta and his children who were now grown and had children of their own.

During that same time Jeremy refused a suggestion from his court appointed attorney that he claim self-defense that night. Instead he made an official confession and pleaded guilty to murder. It was ruled a crime of passion which in Texas is similar to second-degree murder in other states. He was sentenced to twenty years in prison and would be eligible for parole in ten years.

CHAPTER TEN

Life in prison was nothing like you see on television. Much of it, to be honest, was a relentlessly boring routine. His cellmate when he was first imprisoned was Maurice Nicholson who was serving a five year sentence for grand larceny and had just over two years left before his release. He was a pretty good guy who had made a mistake and he sort of took Jeremy under his wing and tutored him on prison life. Yes, there are gangs in prisons but they don't usually pose a threat to other inmates unless you do something to cross them, so lesson number one was don't cross any other prisoners.

Each day primarily consisted of meals, time in your cell and an hour in the yard to walk around or play basketball with other inmates. Maurice advised using the hour to walk around and get some exercise; avoid basketball because sometimes the competition became too heated and led to fights. Fights lead to solitary confinement or even extended time served. Jeremy was allowed to read and often frequented the prison library. It consisted mostly of biographies, adventures, romance and books of faith. Crime novels were not a choice so he focused mostly on biographies and Christian books. Men called Gideons came around every now and then and offered soft cover New Testaments to prisoners and he used this for a daily reading and devotional. He was glad that Maurice was also a believer and they sometimes discussed their faith.

Julie was faithful to come every weekend and visit. These visits were his source of hope and he looked forward to them each week. They discussed the events of the week and also things like financial needs and planning. Since she now had to depend solely on her salary, they decided to withdraw money from their retirement account to pay off the house. This would leave property tax and insurance to be paid each year, but it would reduce her monthly expenses by nearly a third. At her insistence Jonathan came with her on the first visit. He still had the same bad attitude and refused to come after that one visit. Jeremy held out hope and prayed that this would change as he matured.

Jeremy's parents had both died prior to his arrest and so Julie was his only visitor. One day in the middle of the week he was surprised when the guard came and said he had a visitor. He wondered who in the world this could be. He wasn't appealing his case or anything so it wouldn't be his lawyer. Maybe a close friend? But probably not. He was shocked when he walked in the visitation area to see an elderly black man and woman waiting for him. He thought to himself *Oh my, this must be Isaac and Roberta. They probably are coming to let me have it and I guess I deserve whatever they dish out.* He sat down nervously and said, "You must be Isaac."

"Yes I am and this is my wife Roberta. How are you doing in here? Have you got the routine down yet?"

This seemed like an odd question but then no one would know the routine better than Isaac.

"Yes, I have a good cellmate and he's helped me adapt. Isaac, Roberta, I can't tell you how sorry I am about what I did to you; what I allowed to happen."

"You know I've thought about that. I hated you when they first told me I was going to be freed. My family suffered for twenty years. But then I looked at my grandson who's a teenager and I realized how young you were and how scared you must have been. The DA let me read what you said about that night."

"I was young, stupid and scared for sure. But I grew up and I still didn't say anything."

"Yeah, you started a family and probably felt you had too much to lose. Anyway the main reason I'm here is to thank you for finally coming forward. I have cancer and they say it's terminal. Thanks to you I can spend the rest of my time at home with my wife and family. Jeremy, I forgive you."

Roberta had been silent but now spoke up. "Our kids came with me to see Isaac but they never wanted the grandchildren to see him here. So now he's met them and is able to be a Grandpa. It's been a blessing and we do forgive you and thank you for it."

Tears welled up in Jeremy's eyes and rolled down his cheeks. "Oh my, I can't believe this. You people are so wonderful. Those are words I never expected to hear. I don't know what to say."

The visit ended after a few more minutes. Jeremy gave them Julie's phone number and asked them to call her and tell her about the visit. They said they would.

Finally confessing had given Jeremy a measure of relief and freedom but nothing compared to what he felt now. Ironically he felt totally liberated now as he sat in his prison cell. But of course he also terribly missed his life outside of this place. He missed Julie. He missed Jonathan. He missed teaching his students. He missed his friends and church.

About a year into his sentence Julie came in one Saturday. She usually tried to look her happiest and show a positive attitude but today she struggled to do that and Jeremy noticed it immediately. He asked her what was wrong and she told him she had bad news.

He immediately suspected something with Jonathan, but instead she told him that Isaac had died. He had never visited again after that one time but Jeremy felt a real bond between them and was sad to hear the news. But then Julie told him that there was more. She had not felt well lately and had discovered a lump in her left breast. The doctor told her that she had an advanced case of breast cancer. She was to start chemotherapy the next week.

This cut like a knife through Jeremy. He should be there for her at a time like this. She told him that Jonathan knew about it. He had recently graduated from high school and he was obviously upset about the news also. He had promised to go with her to all her appointments and swore he would be there for her throughout the treatment. Jeremy was relieved to hear this and hoped it was the start of a turnaround for his son.

For the next two years Julie bravely fought the cancer. Jeremy was distraught at the change in her appearance. His once beautiful, happy and healthy wife had become very frail and her voice had weakened to a whisper. Most of her hair was lost and she had finally shaved her head and was bald. Seeing her like this mortified him and yet there was nothing he or anyone else could do. She died entering her third year of treatment and he knew that as much as he missed her, she was now in God's hands and was suffering no more. He asked but the warden refused to let him attend her funeral.

*

Jonathan had failed to visit during all this time and Jeremy had almost given up hope. It had now been two years since Julie died. He was surprised when one Saturday the guard said he had a visitor. Walking into the visitation area he hardly recognized the young man sitting and waiting for him. As he sat down, Jeremy observed how much his son reminded him of Julie. He looked very much like her. He had Jeremy's build, but Julie's hair, eyes and face.

"Jonathan, it's so good to see you. I've prayed for so long."

"Hi Dad, I'm sorry I didn't come sooner. To be honest I hated you for a long time. Mom made enough for us to get by but it was hard. She was a single mom and everything was a challenge for us. And then she got sick. It was terrible but I went to every treatment with her. I sat by her in the hospital at the end and watched her die. All I could think was that you weren't there and I was having to do this by myself. I hated you."

"I'm so sorry, Jonathan."

"I know you are. A lot has changed since her death. I finished college. But mostly what has changed is that as I've matured I've seen how much faith Mom had during those times. She stayed positive right up until the end. She said she was in God's hands and that His will was what was best, whatever that was. She never became negative or bitter. We talked about you. She loved you so much. It took me a long time to process what we discussed and my feelings. But now I see that you had tremendous faith also. Despite years of hiding the truth, you finally acted on your convictions and confessed. That must have taken tremendous faith on your part. I could never see it that way before but now I do."

"Oh my, oh my God, I can't believe you're saying that Jonathan. I've missed you so much. I prayed so long for reconciliation and forgiveness from you. Oh son, I love you so much!"

Tears again rolled down his cheek, tears of joy. They continued to talk and Jonathan discussed his future.

"I graduated a month ago and I'm enrolling in seminary, Dad. I plan to become a pastor. And get this, I've been attending our church and the pastor is going to let me serve as an intern while I'm in school. I'm going to work with the youth and on the media team. It's a great opportunity."

Jeremy was so astonished by this turnaround that he wanted to pinch himself and make sure he wasn't dreaming. Jonathan then shared that he had met a wonderful young lady who was also a devout believer and they were getting married the following month.

"I know you can't come but I'm going to record it so you can see the video when we come and I introduce you to her."

"That would be so wonderful. Thanks, son."

Jeremy returned to his cell and sat on his bunk. He thought back on Isaac and Roberta forgiving him, the love that he and Julie shared, the transformation of Jonathan and recalled a verse, Romans 8:28. *"And we know that God causes all things to work together for good to those who love God, to those who are called according to His purpose."* He couldn't help but smile as he laid back on his pillow and pondered this wonderful promise. Yes, God was good.

One Stupid Mistake

by
Bobby J Watson

You have to own your mistakes;
otherwise your mistakes own you.

-Paulo Coelho

CHAPTER ONE

One mistake. One stupid mistake and it ruined my life. It's almost funny to think about it now. People make mistakes all the time. I made mistakes, but nothing like this one. And why? It really made no sense. It went against everything I believed and everything that I loved about life. Twenty three years of marriage and I was nothing but faithful. I loved my wife Evie. I had never loved anyone like I loved her. I still love her. She gave me two wonderful sons and they made my world. I had never even considered having an affair until that one fateful night and it changed my existence to its very core.

I worked in the marketing department of a corporate office. I loved my job. The people surrounding me were good people. Oh occasionally they would invite me to Happy Hour after work. I almost always said no, but once or twice a year I would go with them just to show that I was part of the team. It was the same way with travel. I attended a handful of trade shows during the year and travelled with a team from the department to these shows. They were usually in places like Miami, Las Vegas, New York City and the guys would let their hair down a little at night. They liked going to topless bars or similar joints. They would hoot and holler and throw ones and fives at the ladies working there. I had no interest in this and had a reputation for being a real stick-in-the-mud. While they were out carousing, I was in my hotel room talking to Evie and saying hi to the kids and then falling asleep watching television. Yes, maybe once or twice a year I would go with them just to be part of the group. After all, I did have to work with these guys. And yes, sometimes one of them would hook up with one of the ladies and take them back to their hotel room. I never did. I endured these evenings and suffered through them, just wishing they would end so I could go back to my room. I loved my wife.

So if I could resist these temptations and stay strong, why did I fail at the most unexpected time?

I was excited when the news came that one of the major trade shows would be held in our own city. I wouldn't have to travel out of town and stay in a hotel room. I wouldn't have to worry about going out with the guys. I would work the show and return home to my family every night. How perfect was that?

These trade shows usually featured a large convention center auditorium where various guest speakers would wow the crowd with their talents, ideas, and successes. Outside of the auditorium, the hallways would be filled with booths and displays by various companies vying for the attention and business of those attending. We set up such a booth alongside dozens of other companies that were peddling their wares. This was where I first met Melissa. She was working the booth right next to ours.

Melissa worked for a company that was also local. I had actually seen this company at other shows over the years, but this was Melissa's first assignment at one. She seemed a little uncertain of herself, but she was strikingly beautiful and I knew that she wouldn't have any trouble attracting people to her booth. It may not be fair but yes, beauty does attract people as much as the products being sold. She was of course working with a few fellow employees who were seasoned and would also help her along.

Melissa stood about five feet eight inches tall, with charcoal black hair. Her blue eyes sparkled and highlighted her pert little nose and full lips. She had ample breasts and a pencil thin waist. I was sure that she was either married or had half the guys at her company vying for her attention.

There was actually a lot of dead time at these conventions. Between sessions and at various times during the day those attending would navigate through the hallways and be wooed by those of us working the booths. But they had strict schedules where they engaged in seminars and workshops designed to improve their productivity or increase the success of their company. There was also time spent each day listening to the keynote speakers who had been enlisted as part of the conference. During these dead times we at the booths would sit and wait, sometimes tidying up our areas but often just sitting and talking until the next onslaught of possible customers.

It was during these times that I got to know Melissa a little better. Surprisingly, to me at least, she was more than a pretty face. She was very intelligent and also very informed about everything from politics to sports to business. I actually found myself looking forward to those slow times so that I could visit more with her, and it seemed that she invariably sought me out at these times as well. Some of my compadres noticed this and found it quite amusing, given my reputation for being the dullest guy in the department. I took their jabs with a grin. I fully understood why they would find it so funny.

As much as I enjoyed our conversations though, I was actually shocked on the third day of the show when she asked me to go to dinner with her that night. It had been years since I had been to dinner alone with any female other than Evie. I was so caught off guard that I didn't know how to respond and I mumbled and stumbled and finally agreed to meet her at a nearby restaurant. I was so nervous the rest of that day that I avoided her during down times and found other things to do. What would I tell Evie? I finally called her and told her that I was going to dinner with some of the guys to discuss plans for the final day of the show which was tomorrow. It was the first lie I had ever told her.

I have to admit that I enjoyed that dinner. I was terribly on edge when I arrived, but I tried to hide it and just act like it was no big deal. She led the conversation at first and I immediately started feeling better. I just really enjoyed talking with this woman. I connected better with her than with any of my fellow employees or even friends. After a couple of drinks I felt even better and soon we were having a wonderful evening.

My next shock came when she asked me to come to her apartment. I knew then that it was more than dinner. Why did I agree? Why did I go there? We were no more than inside her living room than her arms were around my neck and we were kissing. She led me seductively to the bedroom where I made love to only the second woman in my entire life. I went home soon afterward, feeling a strange mixture of elation, defeat, and just generally feeling filthy.

One stupid mistake. Why did I do it? I loved my wife. That night changed everything and I could not even imagine the destruction it would bring.

CHAPTER TWO

I hoped it was late enough that Evie would be in bed asleep as I very quietly pulled into the garage and opened the door leading into the house. But no such luck. She was sitting in the den in front of the TV, watching the evening newscast. I felt so guilty, so dirty when she got up and came to me and kissed me. Kissing her had always been one of the joys of my life, but not this night. She must have noticed something because she asked me, "What's wrong, sweetie? You seem upset or nervous or something"? With yet another lie I replied that I was just tired and that the convention sales were down and had me a bit worried. She assured me that it would be okay and we soon went to bed. I lay there until morning. I don't think I slept a wink that night.

I dreaded going to the convention the next day. Melissa was there bright and early and came over to me as soon as I arrived. "I had a wonderful time last night", she said. "I think it's an evening I'll never forget." I tried to keep it low-key like this was nothing out of the ordinary as I replied, "Yes, it was nice". I could tell she wanted to talk more but I made up an excuse about needing to call someone at work and walked off with my cell phone held up to my ear. I went outside and made sure I didn't go back in until some of my co-workers had arrived. I spent the rest of the day doing my best to avoid being alone with her. Finally, after lunch that day, the convention attendees made their final pass through the booths and left to return to their homes across the country. All of the teams started disassembling their booths and I was only too eager to help in any way that I could.

Melissa and her team did the same but I noticed several times that she was looking my way. Finally as we started to make our departure we all waved at the teams adjacent to us and said good luck and good bye to them. I managed to avoid eye contact with Melissa and it felt like I had escaped a near-death experience as I walked out the door.

We all returned to the office and attended a quick meeting to discuss how the week had gone. The convention had actually yielded more sales and appointments to discuss future business than management had anticipated from this convention. They were pleased with the results and the meeting ended with congratulations, atta boys, and high fives all around. Our leader offered to buy the first round of drinks at a local watering hole for all who were interested. I would normally have made an excuse and gone home to Evie, but tonight I made an exception. Guilt still hung over my head and I really wasn't ready to face her again just yet. So I went along, much to everyone's surprise. Not only did I go along, but I had a couple of extra drinks and told some jokes. They must have thought I'd gone crazy and maybe I had. Talk soon turned to the convention and things that occurred there during the week. This quickly evolved into some of the guys discussing the beautiful ladies working the other booths, and especially the young lady next to us. They were certain that I had something going on with her and they ribbed me off and on for the rest of the evening about it. Oh well, better their ribbing than having to look Evie in the eye tonight.

I had called Evie before going to the bar and told her I would probably be late and she should go on to bed at her normal time. I hoped she had done that as I walked out of the bar a little before midnight. As I got in the car to drive home I took out my cell phone and started to lay it in the cup holder next to the driver's seat when I saw that I had received a voicemail. With all the noise inside the bar I hadn't heard the call when it came. I pressed the required buttons to hear the message. My pulse raced and my heart pumped like a piston as I listened. It was Melissa. I had forgotten that I had given her my number early on during the week. I thought nothing of it at the time, just another business contact, another networking reference. Now I heard her voice, "Hey Jarrod, I'm just sitting here in my apartment all alone. I thought you might want to come over. Oh, and I'm wearing a pretty pink negligee that you didn't get to see last night. Why don't you come over and see if you like it?"

My God, what had I gotten myself into? I kept asking myself this and going over my predicament in my mind as I drove toward home. I became so upset that I nearly missed a curve in the road, and I had to pull the car over into an empty grocery store parking lot to settle my nerves. She knew I was married. I had told her. What did she think was going to happen? What can I do to end this? These questions raced through my mind as I sat in that parking lot. Finally I decided that I would just have to ignore her, not answer any calls from her and let this thing die. She was a beautiful girl. Surely she would find someone else when she realized I wasn't playing the game. She was beautiful. It wouldn't take her long. She would forget about me.

CHAPTER THREE

I think that women have some innate sense that tells them when their spouse or boyfriend has cheated on them. Do they smell the other woman's perfume or soap scent? Do they sense betrayal in your actions or words? Do they sense the fear and deception in your voice or your actions? I don't know how it originates, but I'm convinced that they know almost immediately when you have been untrue. And I am especially convinced that Evie has this ability. Even as I lay in bed awake that night after my encounter with Melissa, I felt that Evie knew. She didn't say anything, but there was something different. She didn't snuggle up next to me in bed that night like she usually did. The next morning she was especially quiet as we had breakfast. There was a coldness that I had never felt from her. Was it her or was it my imagination? Maybe it was just my own guilt. I'm not sure, but it was definitely different and not in good way.

To make matters worse Melissa didn't forget me as easily as I had hoped. The phone calls kept coming. She called my cell phone four or five times a day that next week. Each call got more provocative. I also sensed that each call got more desperate. Buy why? I couldn't understand her fascination with me. She could probably have any man at her office that she wanted. I knew she could have had several from my own office. So why me? It made no sense. By mid-week I began to fear that she would show up at my office without any warning and cause a scene if I kept refusing to answer the phone. So when she called later that afternoon I picked up.

She sounded relieved to hear my voice. "Jarrod sweetie, why haven't you been answering the phone? I've been calling all week. You haven't even returned any of my calls."

I lied and said, "I'm sorry, Melissa. I've just been incredibly busy with one meeting after another and follow up work from the convention. It's been crazy over here. So how are you? What can I do for you?"

"What can you do for me? Well, I miss you and I'm lonely every night. That's what you can do."

Fortunately I did have a pretty good excuse. "I am so sorry, Melissa. I hate to hear that but to be honest I'm preparing to go out of town next week for another convention. That's why it's been so crazy around here with two conventions in three weeks." It was very unusual but there actually was another convention. I was not on the team to work that one, but there was no reason she had to know that, and it was a convention that didn't align with the product that her company sold. I had seen the list of businesses showing their wares and hers was not on the list.

"Oh baby. I didn't know that. But I just have to see you before you go. Maybe tonight after work or one evening this weekend?"

She just wasn't giving up and I had to come up with something quickly. "It's going to be really hard I'm afraid. We're working late preparing for next week and this weekend I'm helping my oldest son. He's in Scouts and they have a campout. I volunteered some time ago to help with it." Now I felt even dirtier than before. My son was in Scouts but there was no camping trip. Now I was even using my children to lie and to try to escape this trap I had put myself in. How low could I go?

Her disappointment was evident and I even found myself feeling a little bad for her. Maybe that's why I said what I then said and dug my hole even deeper. "Look Melissa, I know that's not what you wanted to hear but I'll call you as soon as I get back in town after the convention." Why in the world did I say that? No, I didn't want to call her. I never wanted to see her again. What kind of idiot am I anyway?

"Well okay, sweetie" she said. "I guess I'll just have to wait for that phone call then. I'm going to count the minutes until then. I had such a wonderful time the other night and I just can't wait for our next time together. You are so amazing."

I promised I would call again and finally hung up the call. I'm so amazing she thinks? No, I'm not. I'm just an average looking, middle-aged family man. I'm about as normal as you can get. What in the world did she see in me? I kept asking myself that I as drove home that night and was greeted by a luke-warm kiss from Evie. Dinner that night was quiet except for chatter from the boys about school and their baseball practices. Had Evie's radar picked up signals that I had been talking to another woman? Was her sixth sense that good?

Melissa didn't call the rest of that week or over the weekend, which gave me a mild sense of relief. But I knew it was just temporary. She probably wouldn't even call the next week, thinking I was at the convention. But then what? I knew the problem had not gone away. I would have to end this thing somehow.

CHAPTER FOUR

Indeed I didn't hear from Melissa the rest of the week. It felt like the weight of the world had been lifted from my shoulders. I tried to use the time to patch up my relationship with Evie. Did it need patching up? I really didn't know, but it seemed that way to me and so I took her out to her favorite restaurant that Saturday night. As we ordered our food and enjoyed a wonderful meal the conversation seemed to get easier, more like normal. She was very involved with the PTA at our youngest son's school and told me in great detail about a meeting she had attended on Wednesday. It was a planning meeting for a school fundraiser. I couldn't help but reflect that Wednesday was the same day I had talked with Melissa. While I was talking with my partner in adultery, she was working on a school project for our son. That was quite the contrast.

Even though the meal and the evening was the best I had enjoyed since that night with Melissa, I was on edge the entire time. I tried not to show it, but I kept asking myself what would happen if Melissa walked into the restaurant. I was supposed to be on a camping trip with my other son. I really didn't even know her that well but I could imagine her coming up to our table and making a terrible scene. What would I do then? My stomach churned as I pictured this in my mind. I kept looking at the door and Evie even asked me at one point if I was expecting someone else. I assured her that I was not, and then I focused all my attention on her. I locked my eyes on her and determined to not look elsewhere the rest of the night. My stomach churned even more but I apparently was successful and she seemed to enjoy the rest of the evening.

Things continued to go as I had hoped the next week, the week that I was supposedly at another convention. I had feared that Melissa would call in the evening when I would have been in my hotel room, but that didn't happen. I guess she assumed I would be at dinner with my fellow workers and then hitting a bar or club and finally calling it a night. That was the routine for many of the people in my business, and she probably thought that I was no different. Whatever the reason, I was thankful that I got no calls from her that week. But I knew that would not last. She was expecting me to call her when I got back into town. I would have to contact her, but what was I going to say? Somehow I had to terminate this relationship. I didn't want to hurt her feelings, but this had to end.

The team that actually participated in the convention arrived back home Thursday evening and had a meeting the next day to review their results. The time had come. She would be expecting a call from me soon. What was I going to say to her? I dreamed for a moment that she had met her Prince Charming during my supposed absence and forgotten all about me, but then my cell phone buzzed and I saw her name displayed at the top of the screen. Oh boy, I thought to myself. This is it. I still had no plan as to what to say when I answered the phone.

"Oh Jarrod, it's so good to hear your voice darling. I thought this week would never end. Did you miss me, baby? How was the convention?"

I wanted to keep the conversation short. I didn't want anyone to overhear it and get the wrong impression. So I stepped out into the hallway and just said what she wanted to hear. I assured her that I had missed her the entire time too. Yes the convention had gone well but it had been a long week. I told her that I really had to go home tonight and see the wife and kids. I had gotten in late last night and left early this morning so I hadn't really visited with them yet. I even threw in the idea that I didn't want Evie to get suspicious and she might if I didn't come home for dinner and family time tonight.

"Oh, okay. I really can't wait any longer to see you but I guess I understand. For now anyway. But baby, I've got to see you this weekend. I simply must."

I could only say no to her for so long. I didn't want her to start calling me at the house four or five times at night like she had done at the office.

"I know. I understand and I'll come over tomorrow. I'm not sure what all is going on with the kids, but I'll call you as soon as I can and let you know when I can come over. Are you free all day tomorrow?"

"Oh baby, you know I am. Nothing is more important to me than seeing you again. Just let me know when." Then she added alluringly, "And I may have a surprise or two in store for you, lover boy."

I almost choked trying to respond to that. Finally I managed to mumble, "Oh geez I can't wait to find out." Then I made my goodbyes and hung up.

If I felt dirty before, I now felt like I had been dragged through the mud. Lying to my wife, using my kids as excuses and now lying to her and leading her on. I never felt more like a slime ball in my life. A month ago I had been a normal guy, happily married to a lovely woman and father to two great kids. Now I was a sleazy creep, struggling to keep my lies straight.

One thing for sure. This had to stop and it had to stop now. Tomorrow would be the day. I would break it off with her and let the chips fall where they may. I didn't want to hurt Evie and the boys, or even Melissa, but this had to stop regardless of the fallout.

CHAPTER FIVE

The boys both had baseball practice the next day and I spent the morning shuttling between the two practice fields their teams were using. Sitting in the stands and watching them do their drills gave me time to think about what I would say to Melissa. I knew I had to be direct. Confrontation was not exactly my strong suit but I was going to have for force myself to be bold and direct and spell it out to her that this was a bad idea and had to stop. After practices were over we picked up Evie and had lunch at a pizza place that was popular with the kids. It had decent pizza and lots of video and other games. The boys would grab a slice and gulp it down and then head off to another game. Conversation was not easy with loud music playing in the background continuously. But I managed to tell Evie that there was a company dinner tonight and I would have to attend. It was not unusual for the leadership to do this a couple of times a year so the lie seemed plausible. I told her I would cut out at the first opportunity and had no more conventions or other out of the ordinary activities for at least the next three months. I laughed and said, "You'll probably get tired of me hanging around the house." She assured me that would not be the case and held my hand tightly.

About 6:00 that evening I showered and put on clothes fitting for a company dinner, kissed Evie and told the boys goodnight. I had managed to call Melissa earlier that afternoon and told her when I would be coming over. As I drove towards her apartment my stomach began to churn again. I really hated doing this, but I had gotten myself into this situation and I had to get myself out of it. She opened the door so quickly after my knock that I wondered if

159

she had been peeping out of a window watching for me. She threw her arms around me and kissed me long and hard before I could even speak. Slowly we made our way into the apartment and shut the door.

She sat me down on the sofa and perched next to me, kissing me again with her arm around my neck and one hand caressing the back of my head. Finally she stopped long enough to catch her breath. Her smile was from ear to ear and I actually found myself feeling bad that I was going to wipe it off her pretty face. When she tried to embrace me again, I put my arms up and said "whoa, whoa let's take a break for a minute".

She giggled and said, "Oh, okay but I'm just going to eat you up mister".

Oh my, the time for truth was here. I felt like I would throw up. "Yeah, about that. Listen Melissa, we need to talk. This whole thing has gotten out of hand. You're a sweet girl and the last thing I want to do is hurt you, but I can't keep doing this. I have a wife and kids that I love and this was a big mistake that I shouldn't have allowed to happen. But you just came on so strong and I didn't handle it well. I should never have allowed it to start but I did and it's my fault. You're a sweet, pretty lady and there are lots of guys out there. You'll find someone else I'm sure. I'm sorry if I've hurt you but this is the end."

She looked at me and grew more and more pale as I spoke. But then as I continued her demeanor changed. Instead of pale, she started turning red and her eyes became like torches directed at me. The words came rapid fire like an array of darts tearing at my flesh.

"I came on too strong for you? Ha! That's ridiculous! You were the one hitting on me at that convention and you're the one who couldn't wait to get me in bed. Is that what you do, Jarrod? Do you find one at each convention like me? You sure forgot about that wife and kids when you brought me up here and made love to me, didn't you? And you think that now you're just going to walk away? I don't think so."

She then grew quiet and tears started streaming down her cheeks. I felt terrible. I didn't want to hurt anyone. Could I have stated things more delicately? I didn't really see how. Feeling both guilt and compassion, I sat by her on the sofa and put my arms around her.

"Oh Melissa, I do care for you and I'm sorry if I hurt you. I really am, and no I don't pick up ladies at every convention. You may not really know me well enough to see this, but I'm the stodgiest guy there and usually just go to my room every night after dinner. Please believe me. This is for the best, for both of us. You'll find someone else that makes you much happier. You deserve that."

Her crying quietened a little bit and my words did seem to console her. When she spoke this time her voice was much softer, almost a whisper.

"Jarrod, I've never met anyone that I felt so connected to as you. I don't want someone else. I love you like I've loved no man before. I wish you could see that and I think you will someday."

"Maybe you're right, Melissa. I don't know. But I really just have to end this and be true to my family. They don't deserve to have their lives upended. Please try to see that."

She heard my words and looked intently into my eyes, but she didn't really respond. I had said and done all that I could.

"I'm going to leave now. And I really think you'll see that I'm right after a while. I know it hurts now but it will get better. I promise. Goodbye Melissa."

With that I walked myself to the door and left as quickly as I could. I rushed home to Evie and sat on our sofa with her and held her like I never had before for the rest of the evening.

CHAPTER SIX

I didn't hear from Melissa for the next several days and it seemed as if things were returning to normal. I put in my time at the office each day and returned home to dinner and TV with Evie for the evening. Sometimes the boys would join us if a program aired that they liked. I also helped them with their homework and pitched the baseball around with them. Yes, everything was returning to normal and going well. Evie and I even planned for her mother to come watch the boys while we went on a cruise the following month.

Then one morning I was called into the office of my manager. Joe was my immediate supervisor and it was normal to get called to his office occasionally, but I seldom got summoned to Edward's office. He was the manager over our department and Joe's supervisor. When I walked in he handed me a resume and said, "I think you know this person who I interviewed this morning. She worked a booth right next to yours in the convention downtown last month. "

I looked at the resume and nearly lost my lunch. Melissa had applied for an opening at our company and in my department!

I found myself stumbling over my words as I responded, "Oh, uh hmm, yes I think I do vaguely remember her. She's applying for a job here, is she?" I tried to sound incredulous with my question like I was surprised that she would even try to apply with our outfit.

"Yes, she did. And since you know her better than anyone else here I wanted to get your opinion."

Recovering from my initial surprise I looked thoughtful and then said, "Well sir, I have to be honest. I don't actually know her that well, but I just don't see her as a good fit for us. She has no previous knowledge or experience with our type of product. I know she could learn that of course, but my observation of her from the convention was that she didn't play very well with her team there. She just doesn't seem to be a good team player in my view."

"Well that surprises me a little bit. She certainly came on differently in the interview. But you've been with us for a long time Jarrod, and I certainly respect your opinion and appreciate your candor."

"Thank you sir."

"We do have a couple of additional candidates that we're interviewing tomorrow and then we'll make a decision. We definitely need to hire someone and get them trained before we hit the road again."

I thanked Edward again and left his office. What in the world was she thinking? I thought this thing was settled and I couldn't believe she'd try something like this. Fortunately one of the candidates interviewed the next day had some really good experience and made a good impression. They ended up hiring her, much to my relief.

My relief however was short-lived. I feared that Melissa would call me when she learned she didn't get the job, but what she did was far worse. Often on Fridays a group of us from the department would go to lunch together, usually at a gourmet burger place we all enjoyed. Was there really such a thing as a gourmet burger? I'm not so sure that there is, but the burgers were certainly above average and I always enjoyed the bacon cheeseburger they offered. As we sat at our table that Friday waiting for our orders to be delivered, who should show up but Melissa? If I had been eating, I would probably have choked on the cheeseburger when she suddenly walked up to our table and said, "Hey I remember you guys. Several of you worked the booth next to my company's at the convention downtown. Mind if I join you?"

With that she plopped down right next to me as everyone got a confused look on their faces and shifted around the table. She introduced herself and asked how everyone was doing. My teammates responded politely by telling her their names and some said that yes they remembered seeing her before. And then she turned to me and said "And of course Jarrod was there every day. We were bosom buddies by the end of that week. How's it going Jarrod?"

I mumbled something about things being good just as our orders arrived. I couldn't help but notice the looks on everyone's face. There was a combination of mischievously amused and shocked in response to Melissa's description of our relationship. Melissa was bubbling over with chatter and smiles for the rest of the hour, while I sat and ate as quietly as possible. She even informed them that she had applied for a job with our company and failed to get it, but then she continued that she really liked our company and would be applying again in the future. I couldn't wait for this to end.

Finally it did end and we all got up to leave. Melissa said good byes to everyone and then unexpectedly hugged me and said she'd see me later. Eyebrows were now raised. On the way back to the office I assured everyone that I had not seen her since the convention and was as surprised as they were when she appeared at the restaurant. I then sent her a text saying I was coming to her apartment right after work. She replied with a thumbs up and a heart.

I closed the text and started to put my phone away when I saw Jerry with his chin on the cubicle wall that we shared. He was peering right at my phone and had apparently seen the text. Jerry and I had worked together for several years now and he was the closest friend that I had at work.

"Sorry dude" he said. "I was just going to ask if you had read that latest memo on our monthly sales. I didn't mean to pry or anything."

"I guess you saw what I said, huh?"

"Yes, I'm afraid I did and I have to admit I was pretty surprised."

I then confessed the affair to Jerry and how I had been trying to break it off ever since. I shared with him how frustrated I was getting trying to end this thing. He had known me as I said for several years and couldn't believe what he was hearing. He had even met Evie a few times and knew how devoted I was to her. He just shook his head and said, "Man, what a mess. What are you going to do?"

"Jerry, I'm telling you I'm just about at the end of my rope. I don't know what else to do, but I know one thing. I'm ending it tonight, one way or another."

CHAPTER SEVEN

When I rapped on her door that evening she again immediately opened the door. I was prepared this time and held my arms up in front of my face to block any attempt to hug or kiss me. I stormed past her and into her living room and then swung around and shouted, "What in the hell was that? You can't just show up like that and insinuate that we're some kind of item. This thing is over, just like I told you before! It's over!"

"No darling, it's not! I've thought about what you said last time but I know that we're supposed to be together. I love you and you love me. We will be together. I understand that you're upset and that you're concerned about your family, but I can be a good stepmom to your boys. I know I can. So no, I'm not giving up. We are meant to be together and I'm determined to make it happen."

I couldn't believe what I was hearing. Would this thing never end? It had to end, one way or another. I fought to control myself and said, "Melissa, let's sit down and really think about this."

She sat on one end of the sofa and I sat on the other end and looked her intently in the eye. "I know this is hard for you and I hate that I have hurt you so much. I never intended that. But please try to understand. Being with you that one time was the only time I have ever strayed from my marriage. I truly love my wife and kids. I made a mistake, but I don't want to lose any of them. Can you see that?"

"You're a very sensitive, loving and loyal man Jarrod and I appreciate that in you. That's what I see. But I also see that this thing, me and you, is bigger than that. I've known other men but never anyone like you and I can't lose you. I'm not giving up until we are together. I love you like I have never loved anyone."

All hope drained out of me when she said that. I had never felt so helpless in my life. I didn't know what to do. I had no way out of this. I'm not usually that emotional but tears started streaming down my cheeks and I actually started blubbering. She scooted over and held my head in her hands and said, "Oh baby, I know this is hard but it's meant to be."

That's when I totally lost it. I pushed her away and stood up and shouted, "No, no no, this is it! It's over!" She stepped back toward me again but before she could say another word I slapped her hard with the back of my hand. She screamed and I grabbed her by the throat and started squeezing. I squeezed harder and harder and her eyes bulged wider and wider as she struggled to scream again. I don't know how long my hands circled her neck. It was probably only a minute or two but it seemed much longer. When I finally let go, her limp lifeless body fell to the floor.

Oh my God, what had I done! She was dead! I stood and looked at her on the floor for several minutes and then sat down. What should I do now? I can't call the police. This was no accident. No one knew I was coming here. No one had seen me entering the building or her apartment. What should I do? I finally got my handkerchief and rubbed down the wooden arms of the sofa and other furniture. I didn't want the police to find my fingerprints. I was lucky that she didn't scratch me so there shouldn't be any of my DNA on her. I looked around again and left the apartment, rubbing both the inside and outside doorknobs clean with my handkerchief.

Driving home I kept replaying the scene over and over in my mind. I had killed someone. I was a murderer. But she had left me no choice. I was alive but I felt more like the victim in this than the criminal. I felt violated. She had caused all of this. I had tried to end it and she just wouldn't let go. She had stalked me. I was a murderer but I felt a sense of relief in a strange kind of way.

When I arrived home and pulled into the garage, I stood and looked out onto the street for a few minutes. I took several deep breaths and did my best to calm myself. I couldn't let Evie or the kids think something was wrong. Evie was in the kitchen and shouted "You're late" as I walked into the house.

"I know. Something came up at work at the last minute. Sorry, I should have called but I just got busy and it slipped my mind."

"Well okay, but you're in big trouble buddy. We've eaten and you're on your own for dinner."

I thought to myself that she had no idea the trouble I was in but I said, "Oh gee whiz, I am in trouble. I'll have to see what I can scrounge up."

I made a sandwich and grabbed a cola and a snack bag of chips and tried my best to look normal and eat and keep the food down.

The boys came and joined us in the den and wanted to watch a movie. I found it on a streaming app and we all watched it. It would have been such a nice family night on any other occasion. I tried to laugh when appropriate and act like I was enjoying the movie, but in my mind I kept replaying that scene.

I was a murderer but I had no choice. I had to preserve the very thing we as a family were doing right now. I kept telling myself this and then I would wonder if I had overlooked anything that would point back to me. I thought about my cell phone and deleted all the calls and text between us. But what else might I have missed?

CHAPTER EIGHT

The next day was Saturday and it was about as normal a Saturday as you could expect. Both boys had baseball games at the same time at different parks so Evie drove our youngest to his game while I took the oldest to his. I sat in the bleachers and watched the game. Normally I enjoyed seeing a game and especially seeing my son in action. He was pitching today and had a no-hitter through the first three of the seven inning game. I tried to keep up, but inside my stomach was again churning and I kept watching every car that pulled up and every person approaching the seats. I half expected a police car at any moment, but none came and our team won the game 6-1. As was the custom after the game the parents took the boys to a nearby park where they enjoyed sandwiches and other snacks prepared by the moms.

We then returned home to find that our younger team had lost by the same exact score that we had won by. I listened to my son recap the game and his play and assured him that he was a good player. No team always wins in baseball and they would probably do better next weekend. I'm not sure how much my pep talk helped but both boys soon retired to their rooms to play video games and call their friends.

Evie's radar was working well today and she noticed that I was not my normal self. "Is something bothering you?" she asked. "It seems like for the last several weeks you just haven't been yourself. Is everything okay at work? What's going on?"

"Sorry, I've tried not to let it get to me but apparently I'm not very good at that. Yes, we're having some problems at the office. Our earnings have been down for a couple of quarters now and there are rumors of layoffs." This was yet another lie to my wife but it was all I could think of to say. I hadn't been prepared for that question. It had really caught me off guard.

"So are you concerned about your job? Are you in danger of being laid off? "

"I don't think so. I think I'm okay, but I worry about some of the other guys. Most of us have been together several years now and I would hate to see any of them hurt."

"I understand, Sweetie. Try not to let it get you down too much. Even the boys have noticed and asked me if you're sick or something. I'm sure things will turn around."

Great, now I was even making my kids worry about me.

The next day was Sunday and it was even more normal than Saturday. We slept in until about 10:30 and then I took everyone to one of our favorite breakfast places. Both boys had pancakes, while Evie enjoyed scrambled eggs, biscuits with gravy, and sausage links. I'm a corned beef hash guy. I had that and two eggs over easy along with bacon. We all washed it down with orange juice and then she and I got coffee and lingered over it. The food was good but the conversation was even better. We remembered some of our previous road trips, some for baseball tournaments and others for vacations. We recalled especially having fun at Disney World. Who doesn't, right? But we had also had our breath taken away at the Grand Canyon. Evie had been frantic that one of us would fall in whenever we got close to the edge. We all laughed about that. Everyone's favorite however was a trip to the beach in Alabama where we rented a condo and spent the week lying on the beach in the sun, snorkeling and just having fun in the water. That had been a wonderful week. So where would we go this year? Evie and I had our cruise planned, but that was just the two of us. The consensus was that we would wait until the Christmas break for school and go to Colorado to try our hands at snow skiing and stay in a lodge there. I couldn't argue. It sounded great. I just hoped I was around to actually do it.

Things started to change when I went to work Monday morning. Some of my colleagues had seen a report on the Sunday evening local newscast about a young lady being murdered. No identity had been revealed pending notification of the next of kin. But then this morning Patty, an office admin, had watched a morning newscast and it was reported that the young lady was Melissa.

Everyone was startled and several remembered having lunch with her just last Friday. Jerry, my office mate, stared at me with wide open eyes and seemed totally shocked. I had shared the affair with him the same day I went to her apartment. His voice cracked and was just above a whisper when he asked "Jarrod, did you already know about this?"

I assured them that I did not. I hadn't even watched any local news all weekend and I was as surprised and shocked as they were. It quickly became the buzz of the entire office and finally Edward came out and told everyone that he understood their dismay, but we really had work to do. Thank God for Edward. I really didn't want to hear about this all day and I gladly set the example and returned to my cubicle and tried to look as busy as possible.

Jerry eased over to my cubicle and said, "Jarrod, tell me man that this wasn't you. I mean, after what you told me last week."

"Jerry, I promise you that I don't know anything about this. I went and talked with her Friday after work and we settled this thing. She was fine when I left. Just please don't share what I told you about the affair to anyone else." I'd lied to everyone else so I might as well lie to my good friend too.

I then looked the story up online and read it. There were no suspects at this time it said and detectives were exploring the possibility that it was a burglary gone bad. I didn't want an innocent person jailed for something I knew they didn't do, but I hoped the police would stay on the burglary track and not discover anything else.

Lunchtime came and several of us retrieved our lunches from the refrigerator and sat in the breakroom to eat. The breakroom had five tables and chairs, enough to accommodate about twenty people. Talk about the murder dominated the conversation again, although it was quieter this time as people didn't want to draw Edward's attention again. I was asked two or three times how well I knew Melissa and had I seen her since our lunch on Friday. I assured everyone that I barely knew her, just had met her at the convention and that I knew no more about her than they did.

That afternoon was dreadful. I tried to focus on my work but it was nearly impossible. I kept seeing images of Melissa lying on the floor of her apartment with her throat bruised and blue. I thought about claiming I was not feeling well and taking the rest of the day off, but then that would certainly get everyone's attention. That was the last thing I needed.

I attended a weekly meeting where we all sat around a large conference table and discussed the status of our current projects. Twice Joe called my name because I had been asked a question and didn't respond. I was lost in reverie and not really there. Everyone laughed the second time when he said, "Earth calling Jarrod. Jarrod do you read me?" I laughed too and apologized and tried to answer the question he had posed. Finally the meeting adjourned. He pulled me aside as others left the room and said, "Are you okay buddy? The death of this girl has really shaken you up hasn't it?"

"Yeah, I guess it has. It's not that I knew her that well or anything. It was just that one week, but she was a nice person. And I've never known anyone else that was murdered."

"I hear you man. I hope they find whoever did it."

No you don't I thought and returned again to my cubicle. The day was nearly over. Just another hour to go I thought to myself as I looked at the big clock on the office wall. Then the phone rang on my desk and I picked it up. Angela, the receptionist, said "Jarrod there are two police detectives here who want to talk with you."

Two detectives. What did they want to see me about? Had they found something? No, I tried to assure myself that they just learned of my acquaintance with Melissa and want to see if I might know something. I tried to believe this as I nervously and slowly walked to the office entrance.

There waiting for me were two detectives, a woman and man. The woman introduced herself as Detective Carrie Webber and asked if I would come downtown with them for questioning. Her partner introduced himself as James McConnell. They say your life flashes before you just before you die. Mine was flashing before me now as I walked out the door between the two detectives.

CHAPTER NINE

The detectives actually allowed me to follow them to the station in my own car and this gave me a little more hope that this was not going to be a long, intense interview. They ushered me into the building and had me sit down in an interview room with a small table and four chairs. I waited for about twenty minutes then, just sitting by myself in the room. I wondered if this was a tactic they used to soften people up who didn't want to talk. But maybe they just had some kind of paperwork before they talked with me. I really didn't know. Finally Detective McConnell came in and read me my rights, including the fact that I could have an attorney present to represent me. He said this was just a routine they had to follow. I didn't feel like I needed one at the time and told him so.

Detective Webber then joined him and they both sat across from me at the table. I had paid very little attention to their appearance at the office but now, sitting across from me I noted that both detectives looked to be in their mid-30's, but that was where similarities ended. Webber was a thin brunette who wore her hair long and was about 5'6" I would guess. She had piercing brown eyes. She had an air of intelligence about her and was clearly the senior partner. McConnell was a pudgy fellow and was closer to 6' tall. He had hazel eyes and reddish hair that looked like he last combed it a week ago.

Webber started the interview. "So how well did you know Melissa?"

"Barely at all. I met her at the convention downtown a couple of months ago. She was working the booth next to ours and we chatted off and on during the week. I'm surprised you even made a connection between us."

"When was the last time you saw her?"

"I haven't seen her since the convention. Oh, wait that's not true. She ran into a group of us from the office last Friday at lunch and joined us for a few minutes."

"And those are the last times you saw her? Are you sure, Jarrod?"

"Absolutely."

That's when it hit the fan. That's when my boat was sunk. However you want to say it. McConnell then said, "Then how come this text on her phone says you were coming over last Friday evening? And why would the apartment security camera show you entering the building that same night?"

What a great detective I would make. I had thought about the text and calls on my phone, but I had left hers lying on the table next to the sofa without giving it a thought. And I never even noticed the surveillance cameras at her apartment complex. That was when I wised up and asked for an attorney and shut my mouth. Unfortunately it was too little too late. My attorney was Addison Smith, supposedly the best criminal attorney in the city and one of the best in the entire state. He immediately stopped the interview, but they arrested me anyhow. An hour after he arrived I was in a jail cell with three drunks, a robbery suspect and another murderer. Two hours later Evie arrived. I will never forget the hurt on her face as she sat across from me in the visitor area and spoke through the glass window on the telephone.

"You cheated on me Jarrod? And now the girl is dead and they think you did it? Please tell me this is not true. Please tell me this is just a dream, a nightmare."

"Evie, I'm so sorry. It was just one stupid mistake and I tried to end it several times but she just wouldn't let me. "I'm so sorry. I've never loved anyone but you, I swear."

She nodded but the hurt had not dissipated. She said she would work with Smith to get me bailed out as soon as possible. Then she left. I don't think she knew what else to say.

My arraignment was the next afternoon and I was charged with first degree murder. Bail was set at two million dollars. Evie raised the necessary $200,000 for the bondsman by wiping out the majority of my 401(k). I was released and went home but things had definitely changed. There was a telling silence in the house. Even the boys knew that something was off. At bedtime I could tell that Evie was still hurt and not sure what to think or do. I volunteered to sleep in the guest room until she wanted me back in our bed. I never slept in our bed again.

The next several months were spent waiting for attorney motions to be filed, trial dates to be set, meeting with Addison Smith and living like a stranger in my own house. At times I felt like I should just move out, but I hated to give up on my family. Surely this thing would come to an end and life would go back to normal. I hoped for that every day but I knew it was a lie. I recounted the facts of the case to Smith and tried to leave nothing out. He was my only real hope for a future so why would I lie to him? I explained the affair, the aftermath, the ambush at lunch that fateful day and her death in the apartment. I learned to my dismay that not only did they have the text records of my visit that night and the camera shots. She had also kept a journal on her laptop computer. She had written about our meeting and our first dinner together, our sexual encounter in her apartment, and how devoted she was to me despite my efforts to end the affair. She had even journaled that I was coming over that night and she was so excited because she was still convinced she could win me over.

She kept a written journal. Who would have thought?

In light of all the evidence Smith suggested that I try to plea down to voluntary manslaughter, arguing that the death was a crime of passion. With that plea I would be fined and imprisoned for probably five to ten years. That was a much better option than the death penalty he pointed out. I readily agreed to the deal since it was a crime of passion. Smith took our offer to the District Attorney, who surprisingly turned it down. The DA was pretty well known as a hard-ass and he apparently thought he had a strong case. It was also an election year. The case had gained enough notoriety that he wanted to garner all the attention and support he could get from it.

So we went to trial. The DA was absolutely correct in his assessment. He argued that my actions were premeditated. I had deleted any contact with the victim from my phone, I had wiped the apartment clean of fingerprints and DNA, and I had lied about my relationship with her and where I was that evening. Perhaps most damaging was Jerry's testimony. He recapped our conversation that day after lunch and repeated that I had said it was going to end tonight one way or another. Even with that I didn't think the DA's case was that strong, but he convinced the twelve people who mattered. The jury took two hours and lunch before returning a guilty verdict.

CHAPTER TEN

All of this was so long ago, twelve years now but it still seems like yesterday. I recount these events in my mind nearly every day. I appreciate Addison Smith. He has kept in touch with me all this time and tried to appeal the case for numerous reasons. However all of his efforts went unrewarded. We lost every appeal. Still, he has been the closest thing to a friend that I have had. Of course some of the guards are friendly too. The one I talk with the most is Ivan. He comes by and checks my cell several times a week and we've gotten to know each other. He has two sons, just like I did, and they both love to play baseball. A lot of our conversation revolves around that and other family activities that he shares with me.

Evie filed for divorce after my first year in here and shortly after my first appeal was denied. She said that she just could not get past the fact that I had cheated on her. I think she did finally believe me when I said it was only the one time, but even that one time was too much. It hurt so much to lose her. She came and visited me about once a month during that first year, but she never brought the boys. She said she just didn't want them to see me in here. Finally, they both came to see me eighteen months ago. They're grown now so Evie couldn't prevent it. I was thrilled to see them at first but then they told me why they had come. They wanted me to know how I had ruined their lives, making them the objects of ridicule and scorn by their classmates. They were constantly taunted for having a murderer for a father. In addition they said that their Mom had to work two jobs after my conviction in order to keep the house and everything. Her health had suffered because of that. They hated me and wanted me to know that this was the last and only time they would ever see me. The oldest told me he wished I would rot in hell as they left.

Did I deserve all this? I guess I did. But it was funny that after all these years I still felt the same way that I did the night Melissa died. I felt like in many ways I was the victim. She had caused all of this by not listening to me and instead being unreasonable about our affair. Why couldn't she just let it go, let me go? Should one stupid mistake cost a man this much?

I hear footsteps coming my way and then Ivan appears outside my cell, along with another guard. They take me down the hall and to another part of the prison to a small room that I have never seen before. At their direction I lie down on a gurney that is in the room. Unlike most gurneys this one has no wheels, but instead it sits on a large pedestal. The gurney has extensions where I lay my arms and they strap my wrists down. They then strap down my ankles, so I'm pretty immobile now. For good measure however they put a strap across my chest, another across my stomach, one across my waist and finally one across my knees. Next an attendant I've never seen before attaches leads from an electrocardiograph to my chest. There's a large window in the center wall and I think I hear voices behind it, but it's hard to be sure.

Now two more attendants come in and they locate two veins and place two catheters into my body. One of the attendants, a man of about forty with black hair starting to turn gray, explains this as they do it. The warden had also explained to me last night that the catheters are attached to a manifold in the next room that will deliver the three drugs into my body. The first one is an anesthetic and should render me unconscious. As the attendants are doing their job, I'm thinking about the conversation I had with a pastor last week. I tried to be sincere when I confessed my sins and placed my faith in Jesus. I sure hope it worked and I get to meet him soon.

I won't see or feel what happens next but I know what the warden explained. Someone in the other room reads the name of the drug out loud and then the contents of the first and second syringe are pushed in. The syringes are pretty large; they don't want to administer too little, so it takes a minute or two for them to flush. Sure enough after a few minutes, I start to feel sleepy and my vision blurs. I guess the medicine is working. Now they will inject a saline solution into the catheters to clean the IV line for the next drug.

Now after about five minutes they will check to make sure I'm not conscious and then they will inject the second drug. This drug will be a paralytic that will, as the name implies, paralyze me. I'm not sure what the point of that is since I'm unconscious but that's what the warden explained to me. Then after another two or three minutes the third drug will be injected. This one contains potassium chloride, which will stop my heart. They will monitor my heart to see that it flat lines and then log my time of death. The state will have carried out the sentence prescribed by law.

As the first drug takes effect and I know what is coming next, I reflect back one last time on the events that led me here. People make mistakes all of their lives; most of us make some kind of mistake every day. And here I am in this room because of one stupid mistake. One stupid mistake. One stu..... One...

Revenge

by
Bobby J Watson

Before you embark on a journey of revenge, dig two graves.

-Confucius

While seeking revenge, dig two graves – one for yourself.

- Douglas Horton

CHAPTER ONE

Jason Andrews and his wife Carol walked out of the church that cloudy spring afternoon. They were following the casket that was being carried to the hearse by two brothers of Jason, one brother of Carol and three of Jason's cousins. The casket contained the body of their son Damon. They tried to maintain their composure but each of them struggled, especially Carol who was both grief stricken and in a stage of shock as she processed that her only son, indeed her only child was gone forever. She had loved Damon as only a mother could and the thought of losing him was more than she could bear. Jason did his best to comfort her as they took their seats in the limousine that would follow the hearse to Damon's final resting place.

Several friends and family had come by and offered condolences when they stood in front of the casket after the memorial service. They had hugged the couple and offered to help in any way they could. "Call us if you need anything" they had all said, but what could they really do? Damon was gone and was not coming back. Their hurt was real and would not go away. Damon was a senior in high school and was a sweet, considerate young man. Many of his classmates and teachers had also attended the funeral and told Jason and Carol what a good friend and wonderful person their son had been. Several mentioned that he was an extraordinarily sensitive and thoughtful person. Many of the girls wept along with Carol as they remembered their friend.

So, if he was so missed and had so many friends and so large a family, why had Damon chose to end his own life? What had driven him to take the .38 caliber pistol that his Dad kept at home and end his own life? He did indeed have a number of friends and he was not on drugs or anything like that. Like most teenagers he had tried beer and whiskey a time or two, but he had confessed to his Mom that he just didn't care for the taste of it.

He was not a rebellious kid and he didn't run with the wrong crowd or anything. So why had it come to this?

Although they both asked themselves these questions, Carol and Jason both knew what had caused this tragedy. Several boys at school had bullied and harassed Damon from his sophomore year until his death. They had posted a train of comments on social media attacking his physical appearance, spreading false rumors about his sexual preferences and even threatening his well-being. The posts had been extremely vicious and explicit, often containing fake images of their son in horrible conditions. Damon finally reached a breaking point and was found sitting alone and crying in his last classroom of the day by one of his teachers. He showed the teacher the latest photo-shopped image that had been put on social media. The teacher consoled him and told him to report the boys to the Principal the next day.

He had identified the boys the next day to the Principal and the boys were called into his office and given a verbal warning. That however did not stop the cyber-attacks. Damon had become more and more withdrawn and had seen a psychiatrist for depression. It had helped him to some small extent but it did not stop the attacks. Jason and Carol had talked to the school Principal and a school counselor but they had offered very little help. They hoped that he could simply endure his senior year and then go to college which would offer him a fresh start. But as today proved, he reached a point of hopeless despair before attaining that goal.

Jason had managed to access his son's online accounts and had printed examples of the posts that had been made. Damon had deleted many of them but there were still a few that he was able to print. One of the final posts had actually been made that morning. The message infuriated Jason who made sure that

188

Carol never saw it. The post was quite simple. It read "Today we celebrate that the world has one less queer. Adios Damon".

Jason planned to take these printouts to the police the next day and explain the harassment his son had undergone. He would make clear that this had been going on for three years and had led to his son's suicide. He would also refer them to the school officials who had knowledge of these and other incidents. He was no lawyer but he knew that these boys, five of them in particular, had essentially murdered his son Damon. He didn't know what kind of charge they would face but they had to be guilty of second degree murder, manslaughter, or some other felony. Damon deserved justice and he wanted to get it for him.

The hearse pulled into the cemetery and made its way to a freshly dug grave. There was a small area in front of the grave with a tarpaulin set up to protect a dozen or so chairs. It was not raining steadily but a mist and drizzle came and went during the day. The limousine pulled alongside the hearse and Jason and Carol took seats under the tarp as the pall bearers carried the casket to the gravesite. Carol was weeping terribly and all Jason could do was to hold her and offer his handkerchief. The pastor delivered a short homily and one of Carol's nieces sang a hymn that Damon had loved. The casket was then lowered into the grave.

The graveside service had been restricted to family, who now gathered around the couple and hugged them and assured them that Damon was in a good place now. Their faith allowed them to believe this. Damon was now in a safe and loving place and they hoped to join him someday.

The gathering slowly dispersed and Jason and Carol returned to their home. It seemed so quiet now. Would they ever adjust to this new normal?

CHAPTER TWO

Jason was up early the next morning. He had slept very little during the night. He tossed and turned and his mind kept going to the five boys whom he held responsible for his Damon's death. Carol was so emotionally spent and physically exhausted that she had slept hard all night. She barely moved as Jason tossed back and forth. After dressing he went into the kitchen and made coffee. Out of habit he prepared a bowl of cereal and orange juice and sat at the small breakfast table and ate. He then poured a cup of coffee and sat on his back porch and watched the sunrise. Sipping the last of the coffee he returned to the kitchen and rinsed the cup and placed it and the other dishes in the dishwasher.

He walked into his office and opened a manila folder that contained all the material he had gathered to show the police. Reviewing the material brought a new wave of tears to his eyes as he imagined the suffering his son had endured. He had been aware of the toll it was taking on Damon but somehow he never thought that it would lead to the tragic conclusion that it did. Now he rehearsed in his mind how he would present this to the police. Difficult as it may be he would have to maintain his composure and cover each piece of evidence that he had in the folder. He said a silent prayer that he would be able to do so.

Finally he heard Carol stirring in the bedroom. He went and checked on her. She was still in obvious pain and he would have given anything to be able to relieve her of that, but there was very little he could do other than love and support her. He had told her about his plan to go to the police and now he informed her that he was ready to go. She supported him but did not want to go herself. As he headed toward the garage she simply said, "Good luck, dear. They need to pay."

Arriving at the police station he told the officer at the front desk why he was there and the officer made a call to someone and told him to take a seat. Soon a female detective came and met him. Shaking his hand she said, "Good morning, Mr. Andrews. I am Detective Aimee Jinks. How can I help you?"

"Detective, my son Damon committed suicide and we buried him yesterday. He was being harassed by some young men at school and it drove him to do this. I want them held accountable. I have examples of what they did to show you."

Jinks nodded and said, "I'm so sorry for your loss. How old was your son?"

"He was eighteen, a senior in high school."

"I see. So young, that's terrible" she replied and led him to the elevator and then up to the homicide squad on the fourth floor. Jinks dealt with death everyday but when young people were involved, she felt a special anguish. She led him to her desk in one corner of the room and offered him a seat on the opposite side facing her. "So Mr. Andrews you said that you feel certain young men were responsible for this. Can you explain why you feel that way?"

Jason then proceeded to open the folder and went over every message that he had been able to retrieve. He explained that the five boys were also seniors and that these were just a few of the posts that they had made since their sophomore year. Jinks read through them and listened intently to his comments. She shook her head several times and agreed that these were indeed horrific messages. He also shared the incident when the teacher had found Damon sitting alone and crying in the classroom. He gave her the name of the teacher who had found him that day.

She asked if these incidents had been reported to the school and he told her that yes the boys had been called to the Principal's office and given a verbal reprimand but there had been no suspensions and to his knowledge their parents were not informed. He then went on to tell her the name of the psychiatrist who had treated Damon for depression. Jinks nodded her head and took several notes as he detailed all of this. When he was through, she sat and weighed what he had reported.

Finally she said, "Mr. Andrews you have made a convincing case here and I am going to talk to the school officials, especially the teacher and the Principal, and I will also try to talk to the Psychiatrist. He may be reluctant to share anything due to patient-doctor privilege so it might help if you wrote a note that I can show him giving your approval to talk with me. Once I have done that I will go to the District Attorney and share our findings with him. He will ultimately decide to move forward or not. This may take two or three days and I will get back to you as soon as I can."

Jason then gave her his home address, business address and phone number. He stood and shook hands with her and went back home to check on Carol. He believed he had made a compelling case and he also was impressed with the attention that Jinks had given to him. He believed she would follow up and do all that she could.

After checking on Carol, Jason went to the hardware store that he owned in one of the nearby suburbs and opened it for business. He did this mostly just to have a way to pass the time. He also felt he owed it to his two employees to open the business. He had closed it for the funeral and put a sign on the door that it was closed due to bereavement. The next two days seemed like the longest he had ever lived. He spent most of his time during the day at his desk in the back of the store. He spent his nights holding and consoling Carol.

Finally on the third day Detective Jinks walked into the store and they went back to his office. He could tell that she had a grim look but he wasn't sure how to interpret it. Sitting down, Jinks gave it to him straight.

"Mr. Andrews, I'm very sorry to inform you of this but I've talked to everyone as I promised and I met this morning with the District Attorney. While he agrees that this was a great tragedy, he does not believe that there is sufficient evidence to bring charges at this time. "

"No! No! No! That can't be" Jason exclaimed. "They drove my boy to his death. There has to be a law against that."

"Personally I agree with you, Mr. Andrews. But the law on the books that comes closest is Texas Penal Code Section 22.08. It states that if someone helps or promotes the suicide of another they are guilty of aiding suicide. In this case the young men harassed your son but we could find no evidence that they ever suggested that he commit suicide. Without clear proof of intent the D.A. does not feel he can move forward. And even if they were found guilty the penalty is only two years in prison."

Jason simply could not believe what he was hearing. Jinks assured him that if any intent ever came to light she would see that the boys were charged. But without that her hands and the hands of the D.A. were tied. She again offered her condolences and left him sitting at his desk.

It was then that Jason determined that if the state would do nothing about this, he had no choice but to get his son the justice he deserved. Jason was nothing if not a planner. As he thought about his next actions he knew that he could not move too quickly. If one of the boys were harmed the police would immediately make him a suspect. No, he was a planner and he was patient. He would keep up with each of the boys and after a reasonable amount of time had passed he would see to it that they got what they deserved.

CHAPTER THREE

Five years could have been five hundred years. Jason had endured these five years by sticking to his routine. He got up early every morning and had his usual breakfast and then travelled to his hardware store. He greeted customers, rang up their purchases, ordered new inventory, had occasional sales and paid his employees. Some people would have found it monotonous but to Jason it was his refuge. The five years also gave him time to track the lives of the five boys and to determine how he would deal with each one.

Carol on the other hand had found no refuge. Sadness defined her and she simply could not forget Damon and move on with life. She tried support groups and she saw a psychiatrist for depression but she was never again the vibrant and joyful woman she had once been. Jason prayed and tried his best to help her but nothing worked for long and he finally accepted that this was the new her and nothing could change it.

Sean Devers was the first boy on Jason's list. Sean lived in one of the many suburbs that dotted the area. He had gone to trade school and learned to be an auto mechanic. He worked for one of the new car dealers and had married his high school sweetheart. They had recently purchased their first house and planned to start a family soon.

Jason had watched him off and on for the past few months and knew that he normally left the house about 7:15 every morning and returned home when his shift was over at 5:00 PM. He seldom stopped to pick up groceries or anything but instead drove straight home. That is every night but Thursday. On Thursday he went from the dealership to a local sports bar. There he met up with some of his old high school buddies and had a few beers and watched whatever sport was in season on the big screen TV's that lined the walls of the bar. Among these friends were two of the five on Jason's list, but they could wait. He would deal with Sean first.

He had decided that tonight was the appropriate night to initiate his plan. He followed Sean from work to the bar. He didn't have to follow closely, which could arouse suspicion, because he knew where Sean was headed. And indeed he did go the bar just as he did every Thursday night. The bar sat near the end of the street and there was an undeveloped area behind it where a small creek ran through a wooded area. From his earlier surveillance he knew that Sean typically left around 9:00 PM. His friends stayed later but Sean went home to his wife before it got too late.

Tonight when he walked out and started toward his car he was surprised to hear someone call to him. It was a man he didn't recognize who was standing in front of his own car and looking perplexed and upset. The car was parked in the very rear of the parking lot.

"Hey, I was about to go in and ask for help. I don't know what's wrong with this piece of junk; maybe it just needs a jump. It won't start and I'm not very mechanical."

Sean walked over to the man who was probably in his fifties and had graying brown hair and medium build. "Well, I've got some battery cables if that's what is needed but let me take a look first. I'm actually a mechanic."

"Really! Sounds like my lucky night then."

The man had raised the hood of the car and Sean joined him and said, "Hi I'm Sean. Let's see what you have."

"Thanks, I'm Jason and here is what I have" he said and Sean felt something small and round poke into his ribs. Looking down he saw that it was a pistol.

"Oh geez fellow, I don't have any money. Maybe a few ones and you're welcome to them. Please don't hurt me."

"Walk over behind the building, down by the creek. This isn't robbery. This is justice. Do you know what today is Sean?"

"Today? What? No, what do you mean. Today's just another day."

They were between the creek and the building now and no one else was in sight. The music blared from the bar and Jason raised his voice a little so that Sean could hear him.

"Five years ago today, my son Damon killed himself. He killed himself because you and your friends pushed him to it. You bullied and harassed him to death."

"Oh my God! You're Damon's father? Oh sir, you don't know how I've regretted that day. What we did to him was wrong. I'm not that person any more. I have a wife and we're going to have babies. Please sir, forgive me; don't hurt me!"

Sean was actually on his knees by the time he finished saying this and tears were rolling down his face. Jason looked at him and for a moment his resolved subsided, but then he pictured Damon lying in the coffin.

"I wish I could but I've promised Damon that every one of you would pay for what you did."

Before Sean could say another word Jason fired a round into his forehead. Sean's eyes seemed to bulge as he balanced there on his knees for a second before falling over. The gun that Jason used that night was a .357 magnum that had been passed down to him by his father. His father had bought it in the 1950's well before the Gun Control Act of 1968 made registration of firearms a requirement. He had seldom fired it before tonight and the possibility of it being identified and connected to him was almost impossible.

Jason looked at the dead body and tears welled in his own eyes. *What have I done* he thought to himself. Then he looked around to make sure they were still alone. The music was still blaring so he was confident no one had heard the shot which he had deafened by using a silencer.

Leaving Sean lying there he got into his own car and pulled out of the parking lot. He needed to get home to Carol. She needed him.

CHAPTER FOUR

Jason had killed people before but that was different. That had been during times of war as he served in the U.S. Air Force. He had been on several missions in the early days of the Enduring Freedom campaign aboard B-52 Bombers that had targeted Taliban and al-Qaeda targets. He knew that many had been killed during those missions but they were enemies of his country who had aided those who attacked us on 9/11. While he knew that people were killed in those raids he never saw their faces. They were just anonymous casualties who had been killed from the sky.

Looking at the face of Sean Devers had been much different. He couldn't get the image of the pleading voice and tearful eyes out of his mind. Yes, he still believed this was justice but he didn't know if he could maintain the resolve to see it to the finish line. Could he really do this four more times?

Despite these doubts he did determine to surveil the next target and learn what he could about Charlie Campbell. He would keep to his plan and see at the appropriate time if he could see it all the way through. Charlie had also stayed in the area and actually lived closer by than Sean. He worked at an electronics store not that far from Jason's hardware store. He had gone to technical school and worked in the store's support department servicing laptops and desktop computers. He had married soon after graduating from high school but it had lasted only a few years. He now lived alone in a large apartment complex. He maintained a 9-5 schedule at the electronics store and normally had Sunday and Monday off from work.

Charlie was not a social animal and kept to himself for the most part. He was also a creature of habit. Jason observed him for several weeks and the routine was almost monotonous. After work he invariably went by a fast food place, ordered at the drive-through and took the meal home to eat. Not only that but he had the same pattern every week. On Tuesday it was hamburgers, Wednesday was Asian food, Thursday was a sub sandwich shop, etc. Jason observed him periodically for several months and the rotation never changed.

While he was gathering this information Jason acquired another skill. He watched some You-Tube videos and taught himself to pick the locks on doors. Owning a hardware store made it easy to procure the proper set of picks for various locks. He had even gone so far as to pretend to be a potential renter and visit the apartment complex where Charlie lived to see exactly what kind of door lock they used. He was pretty handy with tools and mastered the technique to open Charlie's door pretty quickly. Six months after the death of Sean Devers he believed that he had all the information he needed and he also believed enough time had passed that nobody would connect the demise of Charlie and Sean.

In addition to his lock picking skill he had also completed another critical task. Using a thin steel brush he rubbed the interior of the .357 barrel to change the ballistic characteristics of the weapon. He had read about this and saw that it could work but to be sure he actually wore out two steel brushes on the task. This would make it difficult to tie the two murders together based purely on forensics.

Now the only question that remained was a simple one. Could he do it again? Could he look another human being in the eye and end his life? He really wasn't sure but knew that he had to try.

He believed as much as he ever had that these men needed to answer for the death of his son Damon, and he would either bring about that justice or he would die trying.

He chose a Wednesday. He drove to Charlie's apartment about 4:30 that afternoon and walked up the stairs to the second floor of the complex. He had not observed any surveillance cameras when he had visited the apartments as a potential renter. But just to be safe he wore a baseball cap and kept his eyes to the ground as he moved up the stairs and to Charlie's door. He quickly picked the lock in only a few seconds and walked into the apartment. The living room was nice but furnished very simply with a recliner, a sofa with one end table, a coffee table and a large screen TV mounted on the wall. The adjoining kitchen was small but adequate with a sink, refrigerator, dishwasher, a microwave and an oven that looked like it had never been used. A small breakfast nook with a table and four chairs sat in one corner.

The bathroom and bedroom were also furnished in similar fashion with the necessities but nothing more. There were only a couple of pictures on the walls and they had probably come with the apartment. Jason chose to position himself in the bedroom as he waited for Charlie to arrive. Right on schedule he opened the door at 5:50 PM with a bag containing a plate of Chow Mein and Kung Pao Chicken with a Veggie Spring Roll and some Cream Cheese Rangoons. He balanced a soda in the same hand as he held the keys to the apartment in the other. He sat this on the small counter space in the kitchen and was removing the contents from the bag when he suddenly heard a voice saying "Should I allow you a final meal before your execution?" Startled, he lifted his eyes to a man he had never seen holding a gun just four feet away from him?

"What the hell? Who are you? What do you want?"

"Charlie, you don't know me but I know you. You knew my son Damon in high school."

Charlie's eyes now registered recognition. "Yeah, he was great guy. It was so sad what happened to him. But what's that got to do with me?"

"Oh, I think you know. You and your buddies harassed him and bullied him until he chose to end his life. Remember your old pal Sean Devers? He paid the price a few months ago. Now it's your turn."

"Sean? You're the one who did that? Look mister, I don't know what you think but I had nothing to do with the way they treated Damon. I liked Damon."

Now came the tears as he saw that his words meant nothing. This man meant to kill him. The tears rolled down his cheeks and the mucus ran from his nose as he begged for his life.

Jason wavered for only a second as he watched the young man. Then he quickly put two bullets into him, one in the forehead and one near the heart. He didn't know if any neighbors were home from work yet but again the silencer muffled the noise. He had been careful not to touch anything but wore latex gloves just in case. He now pocketed the pistol, opened the door and removed the gloves. Putting them in his pocket, he proceeded downstairs to his car, still wearing the baseball cap and keeping his head down.

It was now no longer a question of whether or not he could do this. It was just a matter of careful planning and completing his next three missions.

CHAPTER FIVE

Aimee Jinks was an early riser and usually arrived at her desk in the Fort Worth detective squad before the other detectives on her shift. Today was no different as she walked into the large room and headed to the corner where the coffee bar was located. She brewed a pot of coffee and poured herself a cup of the black liquid. She went to her desk and sat down and then opened an electronic copy of the local newspaper on her laptop. Sipping from the hot cup of java she perused the paper until she saw an article about a murder in one of the nearby suburbs. A young man named Charlie Campbell had been murdered in his own apartment. He had been found when his employer became concerned about his unscheduled absence from work. He said that Charlie was good to call whenever he was sick or had another reason to not report to his job. The employer went to his apartment and asked the manager to open the door to Charlie's apartment. They found him shot to death in what appeared to be execution style. There was no sign of robbery or a struggle.

The suburbs sometimes asked the Fort Worth police department for help with major crimes since they had more detectives and other resources. But this murder had occurred in one of the larger suburbs, one that had its own homicide detectives and they did not ordinarily ask for assistance. But as Jinks read about Charlie Campbell something ticked in her head. Charlie was a local man who had attended one of Fort Worth's high schools before moving to the suburb. Jinks read the article twice and something about it sounded familiar to her but she couldn't identify it. Oh well, maybe it would come to her. Meanwhile she had her own homicides to investigate.

At the same time Jason Andrews was sitting at his own desk in the back of the hardware store reading the same article. He felt pretty certain that he had left no clues behind and there was no known connection between Charlie and himself. Just as with Sean Devers he kept seeing the face of his latest victim, but it was not as bad as with the first murder. He thought to himself that *I guess you can get used to anything given enough time and repetition.*

Jonah Ryan was his next target. Jonah had moved to the town of Weatherford and established an insurance agency. Weatherford was about thirty-five miles away. It was a nice small town with about 30,000 people and was the county seat of neighboring Parker County. He was married with two small children and had done pretty well for himself. Jason had researched his social media accounts as a first step in learning more about Jonah. He didn't friend or follow him but he would periodically look at his posts to learn what he could. He would continue to do this for the next couple of months before engaging in more direct surveillance.

A more immediate concern for the moment was Carol. Her depression had deepened and now she was seeing a psychiatrist on a scheduled basis. Jason had not seen any real improvement with her and feared that she might do something drastic. *What would he do if she committed suicide?* She had been such a happy person until Damon's death that a thought like this would have never entered his mind. But now it had become an all too real concern. He tried his best to support and comfort her but his efforts were pretty futile. He had suggested that she get a job, thinking that it would offer her a refuge from her thoughts and she might even make friends with some of her coworkers but he had been unable to convince her. He loved her so much. What would he do if something happened to her? One thing he knew for sure. If something did happen to her it would be the fault of those five boys just as much as Damon's suicide.

Five months after Charlie Campbell's murder, deer season began in Texas. Deer season was an obsession for many Texans. When it arrived in the fall many hunters took a week or even two off to pursue the animals. Many had cabins near the woods and parties of several men would gather for the hunt. At night they would sit around a campfire and spin yarns of past conquest. Then they would rise early before sunrise and station themselves in blinds hoping to spot their prey and bag a trophy. Jonah Ryan was one of those enthusiastic hunters. He had a cabin in the woods outside of Weatherford and always left the office in the care of his assistant during that first week. Unlike many of the other hunters however, Jonah had grown to enjoy the solitude and quiet of that time and stayed by himself in his cabin. He dealt with people on a daily basis as an insurance agent. This week he gave to himself and was happy to see nobody except the deer he hunted.

Jason had learned Jonah's habit as he delved into his life and stationed himself behind a tree that morning at 4:00 AM. Jonah's cabin was thirty yards away and Jason had a .30-30 Winchester rifle loaded and ready for him to come out that morning. He was a fair shot with a rifle but had practiced at a range the last two months to improve his marksmanship.

Jonah opened the cabin door a little before 5:00 AM that morning. He had a deer blind he intended to go to and felt he had a good chance of bagging a buck that morning. The blind was about half a mile through the woods from the cabin. However Jonah made it only about ten yards that day. A bullet from Jason's rifle tore through his heart and he fell to the ground, dying instantly. Jason walked up and ensured that he was dead and then trudged a mile through the woods to his own vehicle. Jonah might not have gotten a deer that morning but Jason had bagged his prey.

CHAPTER SIX

Jason felt a combination of remorse and accomplishment. He had completed sixty percent of his mission with three of the five people responsible for Damon's death now in their own graves. He had become somewhat but not entirely desensitized to the executions he had carried out. He refused to call them murders because he believed they were entirely justified and rendered justice to the guilty. If he had to answer someday before God or man he would do so, but not with any sense of wrongdoing. And yet there were moments when a feeling of remorse crept into his consciousness. He saw the faces of all three men on a daily basis, or more often on a nightly basis as he lay in bed unable to go to sleep. His remorse came more from acknowledging that they had parents, wives, and children than it did from any sympathy for the men themselves. He was convinced they had received the justice they deserved.

Meanwhile Carol's depression continued. There were days when she seemed to show some improvement, but more often it appeared that the therapy was doing very little for her. The psychiatrist explained to him that before she could really move forward she had to decide that she wanted to feel better and she had never really made that internal decision. Jason did his best to encourage her, telling her how much he loved and needed her. She heard his words but sometimes he thought it was like there was some kind of invisible shell around her and nothing could penetrate that barrier.

When it seemed that she could get no worse, she did. Carol developed a cough and wheezing that would not go away. They tried cough syrup and over the counter cold medicines but they did not help and her symptoms got increasingly worse. Finally he took her to the ER one night where they made X-rays and the doctor on duty told them that she had a case of pneumonia. This seemed odd since they had both had vaccines, but of course sometimes vaccines did not prevent certain strains. The X-Ray also revealed a mass on her right lung and so the doctor recommended they admit her to the hospital for more tests.

After a series of CT scans, MRI's, PET scans and other tests the hospitalist said that she had cancer and recommended an Oncologist. The Oncologist did his own round of tests and concluded that she had cancer in her left kidney as well as her right lung. This made it stage 4 cancer, but he believed she could still be successfully treated. He recommended an immunotherapy regimen. Carol was given two different drugs, Ipilimumab and Nivolumab. These drugs were designed to super charge her own immune system so that it could target and kill the cancer cells. One good thing about immunotherapy was that it had very few side effects compared to chemotherapy and the side effects were generally much milder.

Jason prayed every night that these drugs would work. He had already lost a son. He simply could not lose Carol too. He still went to the store every day but he spent less time there, leaving much of the responsibility for the business in the hands of his assistant manager. He did all he knew to do to comfort and aid Carol. Fortunately she was not in a lot of pain from the cancer but he knew that could change quickly if the treatments didn't work.

Despite the issues with Carol's mental and physical health he stayed true to his mission. However he determined that since he had executed two of the culprits in the last eleven months, he would slow down his pace and let more time pass before targeting the next one. This gave him more time with Carol and also more time to plan the next step in his mission.

Carol's treatments appeared to work well for the first several months, but then they took a turn and the Oncologist recommended that they switch to chemotherapy. The cancer had spread to her other lung and was now growing more aggressively. Shortly into this new treatment she began losing her hair and often suffered from an upset stomach. Delaying the next execution let him spend more time with her during this crucial period. It also enabled him to plan in more detail.

This plan was different than the others because he intended to finish the mission and take care of both remaining targets in one step. Danny Jeffers was the only boy who had moved away from the area. He now resided with his wife in Houston Texas. The other remaining target was Jack Middleton, who ironically now worked for Jason and was in fact the assistant manager who was watching the business while Jason attended to Carol.

CHAPTER SEVEN

The fact that Danny Jeffers lived in Houston presented some difficulty in formulating a plan. With the others he had been able to surveil them pretty easily since they had all stayed in the greater Fort Worth area. Fortunately however it wasn't a major problem. Jason would simply arrange periodic "buying trips" for the hardware store and then spend a night or two in Houston where he learned the habits of his next victim. While he was away he put Jack Middleton in charge of the store. He also engaged a hospice company to watch over Carol during these absences. Her condition was rapidly deteriorating and he knew that he had to prepare himself for the inevitable regarding her.

Jason was a little surprised to see what a normal and tranquil life Danny was living in Houston. He worked in the IT Department for a large corporation whose headquarters were in Houston and he had a nice home nestled in the suburbs. He and his wife had no children but planned to start a family soon. He learned this one day as he followed Danny to lunch and sat in a booth behind him at a hamburger joint. Danny was with a co-worker and they both discussed their plans for the future. Danny revealed that they wanted two children, a boy and a girl but two boys or two girls would certainly be okay as well. Jason hoped that he finished his business with Danny before his wife got pregnant. There was no need to make her life harder by making her a single working mother.

His shadowing of Danny revealed a pattern that seemed pretty stable. Most days Danny simply went to the office, ate lunch either at the office or at a local restaurant, and then returned home. He did not have a weekly card game, night out with the guys or clandestine affair that deviated from the plan. However on Wednesday nights his wife always went to mid-week church services. She was apparently in the choir and attended practice after the mid-week service concluded. She usually returned home between 9:00 and 9:30 that night. Danny, on the other hand, did not try to attend the service. It would have been difficult for him to arrive on time because of the Houston traffic. Instead he simply went home, usually getting there between 7:00 and 7:30. This gave Jason the opening that he needed.

Houston is the fourth largest city in the U.S. with nearly 2.5 million residents. At its current growth rate it will overtake Chicago for third place in just a few years. So understandably it has a number of convention facilities as well as the hotels and restaurants to support those conventions. In fact the largest buying convention for hardware stores was scheduled to be held in Houston that summer. This gave Jason the perfect opportunity to be in the city for a few days and complete his plans for Danny Jeffers.

He completed his last trip there a month or so before the convention. Everything was going according to plan. The one thing that could complicate matters was Carol. She was getting progressively worse and the oncologist held out little hope that she would survive the summer. Carol meant everything to Jason and if her condition worsened he would delay his other plans to be there for her. He could always devise another plan for Danny if it came to that.

But her condition also meant that he was spending more time at home. Even though the hospice nurse was there and doing a wonderful job, he wanted to be with Carol as much as possible during this time. He leaned more and more heavily on Jack

Middleton to run the store and he had to admit that Jack was a great help. Jack had actually been the ring leader in the group's tormenting of Damon but he had changed a lot since those high school years. Jason had to admit that Jack had turned out to be a pretty nice guy. Not just a good employee but a nice young man who had not yet married but was engaged to a beautiful young lady named Stephanie. They planned to marry sometime around Christmas of that year.

Jason often surprisingly found himself enjoying his time with Jack at the store, but then he would remember what Jack and his buddies had done. No matter how much he had changed, he needed to pay for his crime and Jason would never forget that. There was simply no room for forgiveness. And as his plans had come together he had arrived at a surprising and unexpected decision regarding both Danny and Jack.

CHAPTER EIGHT

Jason had planned to simply kill Danny and then Jack just as he had done with the first three, but the more thought he put into his plans he decided on a different course of action. Why not take care of two bullies with one murder?

Jack had been a good employee for a few years now and he was a very capable assistant manager. Jason was genuinely grateful to Jack for taking on more responsibility, especially this past year when he had needed time off to take care of Carol. When he called Jack into his office that morning, he saw the apprehensive look on Jack's face and quickly reassured him that everything was okay.

"Jack, the truth is that you have done a really terrific and needed job this past year. I'm not sure the store would have survived without you. "

"I appreciate you saying that Mr. Andrews. I know that it's been a hard year for you and I was glad to help in any way that I could."

"And you have been a great help, Jack. So I've decided to reward you a little and give you a step up in responsibility. You know the big buyer's convention is in Houston this year, not the most scenic and captivating place in the world but the convention center is really nice and they have some great bars and restaurants nearby. So I'm sending you there this year instead of going myself. Partly, that's so that I can stay near Carol. I've travelled enough this year. But mostly it's just a good way for you to gain some valuable experience and have a little time away. "

"Gee Mr. A. I don't know what to say."

"Nothing to say. Here is your round trip airline ticket to Houston. I've also reserved a room for you at the hotel right across from the convention, and I can assure you it's a first-class hotel. I want you to enjoy it and of course pick up some good buys if you can. It's a great opportunity to network and meet some people. I only ask one thing. On Wednesday evening I need you to grab room service at your hotel and wait for a call from me. I want to hear your progress but I may have some specific buys that I want you to make the next day. That's the last day of the convention and there are usually some really good deals then."

"Will do sir! And I really appreciate this opportunity. I won't let you down and I'll wait for your call Wednesday evening."

Actually there would be no call. He just wanted to be sure that Jack was not out having dinner and a good time with some newly made friends who could give him an alibi for that night.

The convention was still a month away and the primary thing that could interfere with Jason's plan was if Carol's situation deteriorated. But fortunately she did not take a down turn and so Jason proceeded with his plan.

Jack had one bad habit that worked perfectly into Jason's plan. He was a smoker and had a corner in the back of store where he sat and smoked during his breaks. He kept an ashtray there on a little table and would empty it when it started to overflow. He also kept a cigarette lighter on that table. One day after the store had closed and Jack had gone home, Jason took a pair of tweezers from his pocket and took three cigarette butts and placed them in a clear sandwich bag. On the day that Jack left for the airport to attend the convention, Jason used a cell phone registered to the store and texted Danny's number. He explained that this was Jack and that he would be in Houston that week and hoped they could get together. He said that he had something he wanted to discuss with Danny. Jason never bothered to see if Danny answered; he just wanted the text to be found later on the phone.

He then went to the smoking corner and using a handkerchief he carefully took the lighter by the corners and put it in a similar bag.

The convention opened on Monday and got into full swing on Tuesday. Jack actually texted him and told him how much he was enjoying it and mentioned some possible buys that Jason responded that he should make. Then that Wednesday he closed the store a little after noon and got into his car and started on the four hour drive to Houston. If anyone should ask about the early closure, he would simply explain that he had needed to take off and tend to his wife who was having a bad day.

He got to Danny's house about 6:15 that evening and parked along the other side of the street. He had observed that Danny invariably parked his car on the right side of the driveway and opened the front door to enter the house. His wife would later park in the garage. Tonight when he opened the door to enter the house, he suddenly felt something poking his back and a man telling him to keep still and go on inside. Then the man told him to sit down on the sofa. He did so and then looked at the man, who had not bothered to cover his face. He looked vaguely familiar but Danny did not recognize him.

"Look, take whatever you want. Just take it and leave. I won't call the police. Just don't hurt me, please!"

"I wish it were that simple, Danny" the man said.

Danny was surprised that the man knew his name. Who was this? But then the man explained that he was Jason Andrews, Damon's father. Danny went white as a sheet and fought for words to say to this man. But Mr. Andrews did the talking. He explained that he knew why his son had killed himself and who had been involved in bullying him until he could no longer live with it. To

Danny's further shock, he then told him that three of the five had already paid for their crime. Only Danny and Jack were left.

Danny then found his voice and pleaded and begged for mercy just as the others had done. He was so sorry for what they had done, but he had changed. He had a wife and they planned on a family. Desperate for words he even promised to name one Damon if they had a boy. Jason listened and let him have his say, but then he ended the conversation.

"I know you have changed but that doesn't make up for what you did and the torment that my wife and I have been through."

He shot Danny once in the forehead and once in the heart. He then got a small dish from the kitchen since there were no ashtrays in the room and emptied the bag of butts onto the dish. He then laid the lighter down beside the dish.

Getting in the car for the long drive home, he hoped that he had done enough and that justice would now be served.

CHAPTER NINE

Jason knew that it was very unlikely that the local news would have any kind of story on the murder of Danny Jeffers. The Dallas-Fort Worth or DFW area had more than enough violence of its own to fulfill the needs of local TV and newspapers. Only the most heinous murders from another market would appear locally. So he scoured the internet and finally found a report two days after the incident. Police seemed to think that it was probably a home burglary gone bad, but the case was too new to draw any conclusions. He continued to follow what news there was on the story but apparently Houston had plenty of violence to report as well and new information soon disappeared as more recent and eye-catching crime took the forefront.

Two weeks passed and then one afternoon two men wearing suits entered the store and asked to speak to Jack Middleton. When Jason asked what it regarded they flashed Texas State Police credentials and said they just had a few questions for Jack about an incident in Houston. He called for Jack who was in the back of the store taking a break. When he appeared and saw who the men were, he looked totally lost. He had no idea why any police, much less state troopers, would want to speak with him. They began by asking Jack if he knew Danny Jeffers to which he replied that yes he went to high school with him, but had not seen him in years. They then asked if he was in Houston two weeks prior. Danny now looked totally confused and looked to Jason for help.

Jason had given this a lot of thought. How should he react when police came and questioned or even arrested his employee? He had decided that the best move was to act just as surprised as Jack and offer to help any way that he could. After all, if what he had planted was sufficient evidence then no amount of help that he offered now would make a real difference.

"What is this about?" he asked the detectives.

"I'm sorry sir but we can't go into details on an open investigation."

They asked Jack again and he replied that he had been in Houston for four days at a convention but that he had not seen Danny during that time. He didn't even know that Danny lived in Houston.

The detectives looked at each other and the one who appeared more senior nodded to the younger one. This contradicted the message they had found on Danny's phone, telling him that Jack would be in town that week and wanted to meet with him.

"Jack Middleton, you are under arrest for the murder of Danny Jeffers. You have the right to an attorney..."

The spiel went on but Jack looked totally shell-shocked. He finally nodded when the detectives asked for the third time if he understood his rights.

Jason had to admit that he found the whole thing nearly as unnerving as Jack did when it played out in real-time before him. He did manage to ask the detectives where they would take Jack and he told Jack to answer no questions. He said that he would help him get an attorney.

Perhaps the most difficult thing was calling Jack's parents and telling them what had happened. Jack's father was caught totally off guard by this news. He was silent for a long time and then when he spoke, his voice seemingly broke with each word. It was all he could do to prevent himself from bursting into tears. He finally said that he and his wife had a friend who was a criminal defense attorney. They would call him, though they had never dreamed they would need his services. Jason said that he would close the store and meet them where Jack was being held. Hanging up the phone, he just stood there for several minutes. He was accomplishing his mission. Everything was going according to plan. And yet he was stunned that this was affecting him so much. He had walked away from four murders and learned to feel very little, but now he was seeing the effects of his work first-hand and it left a sour feeling in the pit of his stomach.

Jason was even more touched as he entered the police station and met the parents. They were totally devastated. When the attorney arrived, Jason grabbed him and volunteered that he would post any amount for bail. The attorney then went inside where the detectives began questioning Jack. When he came out the attorney reassured the parents but privately told Jason that things did not look good. At this point Jason was unsure how to process that information.

Because it was a first-degree murder case bail was denied. Jack stayed in the Harris County jail for the next six months. His parents took an apartment in Houston and visited almost daily and Jason tried to see him every couple of weeks. He was doing an excellent job of playing the role of a sympathetic employer. Seeing the toll it was taking on Jack's parents was heart-wrenching. The mother was pale as a sheet every time he saw her. Both she and her husband were visibly losing weight. Jason began to hope he would simply not see them whenever he went to visit.

Finally the trial date was set and a jury was selected. The evidence was all circumstantial but overwhelming. He was definitely in

Houston at the time of the murder. He had texted Danny that he wanted to visit him about a matter and this probably provided motive, although they never learned what the matter was actually about. The DNA evidence from the cigarette butts and the lighter proved that he was at the Jeffers home. The murder weapon had never been found. Search warrants had been served at Jack's residence and at the hardware store but the searches had turned up nothing. Still there was just too much when you added it all up and Jack had no answer for how the evidence got there.

Indeed Jack was totally mystified that someone had obviously framed him but he had no idea who would do such a thing or why. It almost seemed comical to Jason that Jack never seemed to suspect that he was someone who could easily have obtained and planted this evidence. But instead Jack trusted him completely throughout the process and relied on him to help keep up the hopes of his parents.

Finally the verdict came in. The jury unanimously found him guilty. Jason, as well as Jack's parents and a number of friends testified to his good character during the sentencing phase. They still could not believe he would do such a thing. He was just not capable of murder. Unfortunately for Jack, the jury was swayed more by the callous and calculating nature of the crime than they were by the testimony of friends and family. Jack was sentenced to death by lethal injection.

Jason left the courthouse that day with tears swelling his eyes. But even he was unsure if they were tears of joy for handing out justice for Damon, or tears of regret for what he done to these five men and their families.

CHAPTER TEN

In the months following the trial and Jack's sentencing Jason tried to focus on two things: taking care of Carol and taking care of the store. He hired a new young man to replace Jack. Blake was a nice young fellow and was a hard worker. He was eager to learn the business and to take on more responsibility. He was just the type of employee that Jason needed and he should have been grateful to find him. But every day he found himself remembering that Jack had those same qualities. And to be truthful, he was simply not succeeding in his efforts to focus on the business.

So about three months after the trial was over, he sold the store to a national chain. He got a nice purchase price and he insisted that as part of the deal the company would retain Blake and enroll him in their management training program.

This meant that he could focus full-time on Carol. The hospice nurse still came by each day but Jason took on more of the household responsibilities. He prepared all the meals and did the dishes and the laundry. He saw that she took her medicines on time. This went well at first and seemed to give him more sense of purpose. But then one night Carol woke up and started coughing up large amounts of blood. He called the oncology center's 24-hour number and was told to get her to the Emergency Room immediately. He did so and they were able to stop the bleeding but they kept her as an inpatient for several days.

After switching from immunotherapy to chemotherapy she had initially shown some progress despite the terrible side effects.

But then she had again started to decline and the oncologist told Jason that while there was hope, he should prepare for the worse. Carol was a fighter and she bravely faced this challenge but four months later she lost the battle. Jason was devastated. He was now all alone, without Carol and without Damon.

Carol had many friends. She had been much more involved in their church than Jason and the memorial service was packed with those who remembered her. They all wished him well, offering to help however they could. But just as with Damon, what could they really do? He tried to move on with life. He joined a gym and went almost every day where he worked out but more importantly he met other people. He had promised Carol that he would not isolate himself. He also became more involved in church and attended a weekly men's bible study where he made new friends. While doing all of these things, he also kept track of Jack.

There is nothing swift about the death penalty. Jack's attorney filed appeals which took months to be heard and yielded nothing. He was on death row in Huntsville Prison and it usually took ten to twelve years after sentencing before executions were carried out. Jason debated whether to go see Jack but had difficulty working up the nerve.

Time passed as days and weeks and months and even years went by. Jason maintained his routine with the gym and church. He watched too much television and had little to do other than these activities. One day as he was on the elliptical machine at the gym he suddenly felt weak. He lost focus and tripped over his own feet, falling to the floor. Attendants rushed over and one of them called 911. They laid him on the floor and raised his head until the ambulance arrived and took him to the hospital.

The doctors at the ER revived him and he spent several days at the hospital. A cardiologist came to visit him and he went to the specialist's office after his discharge. They ran several tests before confirming that he had congestive heart failure. The cardiologist was blunt. He told him that because Jason was also a Type 2 diabetic he might survive five years or even ten if he adhered to the treatment plans. But because he was diabetic and also had a history of high blood pressure, the time might be less.

Jason did well with the treatment for the first several months but he found it hard to keep motivated. Depression became more and more prevalent and he struggled to find a desire to live. Finally he decided that there was only one thing he really wanted to live to see and that was the execution of Jack Middleton. It was then that he determined the time had come to go see Jack.

Jack was surprised to see him but happy to receive any visitor. They each updated the other on how they were doing and chatted for a few minutes before Jason worked up the nerve to say what he had come to say.

He didn't think they were being recorded but wasn't sure. He did know there were guards watching them and all the visitors. So he whispered almost inaudibly to Jack.

"Jack, do you know why you are here? Do you remember what you and your friends did to my Damon? How you bullied him to death? They have paid the price and now so are you."

Jack just stared at him for several seconds, though it seemed much longer.

"Mr. A., you did this? What have you done? I told you how sorry I was about that and I begged your forgiveness. I begged God's forgiveness. We hurt Damon but look at the lives you've destroyed. Not just the five of us, but our parents, wives, children! And we're the monsters? No Mr. A., you're the monster!"

Jason left that day more conflicted than ever. This had not helped at all. Was Jack right? He thought about what Jack had said and tears again swelled his eyes, this time rolling down his cheeks. Had he gotten justice or was he really the monster?

Jack of course relayed this new information to his attorney because a week later a private investigator came and questioned Jason about the conversation. Jason denied it and nothing more seemed to come of it. It was just his word against that of a convicted killer. Jack's future date with lethal injection still loomed ahead. That time grew closer and closer and Jason hung on day by day awaiting it. However Jack had gotten to him and he kept thinking about the families harmed by his actions.

Jack's execution was one scheduled one month away and Jason's condition worsened. He was admitted again to the hospital. The question plagued him: *had he done the right thing or had he just added to the injustice in the world*?

He had developed a habit of reading verses from his bible each day. Actually it was not his bible, but Carol's. He enjoyed seeing what she had underlined and highlighted in her own reading. Sometimes he followed specific bible plans and at other times he just opened the book and read from that page. That is what he did today as he lay in his hospital bed. The verse highlighted on the page was from the New Testament book of James.

Chapter 2 and verse 13 read: *For judgement will be merciless to one who has shown no mercy; mercy triumphs over judgement.*

224

He kept thinking about this verse and what it said. He then wondered what had prompted Carol to highlight it. He also kept looking at the hospital room phone next to his bed. Should he call 911 and confess while there was still time or should he see his plan through to the end? Finally he reached for the phone but found it was just out of reach and he was too weak to retrieve it. He pressed the assistance button and a nurse answered.

"What do you need, Mr. Andrews?"

"I need the phone and can't reach it. Could you please come get it for me?"

ACKNOWLEDGMENTS

These stories would not come together without the help of my wife of over 50 years Priscilla and of my daughter Melinda Mabry who read my stories, offered valuable feedback and did the initial editing. Also, special thanks to Rachel Bostwick for formatting the book and creating the cover design.

ABOUT THE AUTHOR

Bobby Watson earned B.A. Degrees in English and History at the University of Arkansas where he also earned an M.A. in History. He is a retired computer software consultant who travelled extensively throughout the USA and began writing memories of his younger years as a hobby, thinking his kids and grandkids might want to read them someday. He then expanded to writing crime novellas and short stories and shared them with friends who encouraged him to publish these stories. He finally decided to take the plunge and the result was his first published book *Twists of Fate*, a collection of five crime stories. A person of faith, Bobby woke up one morning with the idea of writing a book based upon a particular biblical story and the result was *The Testing*. It was well received by his pastor and other friends and led to him writing additional stories based on the parables of Jesus. *The Testing* and these other stories comprise his second collection titled *Crossroads of Faith*. His latest collection of five crime stories is entitled *Deadly Choices: Tales of Deceit and Revenge*.